PENGUI.

THE HEART OF SUMMER:
STORIES AND TALES

Danton Remoto took up publishing studies at the University of Stirling (British Council scholar) and world literature at Rutgers University (Fulbright scholar). He was also an Association of Southeast Asian Nations scholar in English Literature at the Jesuit-run Ateneo de Manila University and a research scholar in Asian Literature at the National University of Singapore. He has worked as a publishing director at Ateneo, head of communications at the United Nations Development Programme, TV and radio host at TV 5 and Radyo 5, president of The Manila Times College, and head of school and full professor of creative writing at the University of Nottingham, Malaysia. He has published twelve books, including the acclaimed novel, *Riverrun*. He translated the 1906 novel by Lope K. Santos, *Banaag at Sikat*, into English (*Radiance and Sunrise*) for the Southeast Asian Literary Classics series, as well as the novels by the Philippine national artist, Amado V. Hernandez, *Ibong Mandaragit (The Preying Birds)* and will publish *Crocodile's Tears (Luha ng Buwaya)*. He has also been writing and editing for the Philippine press over the last thirty years and has published more than 3,000 columns and feature articles. He is currently the News Editor of *The Manila Times*, the Philippines' oldest newspaper that was founded in 1898. He is a co-editor of *Ladlad: An Anthology of Philippine Gay Writing* in 1994, which was the first multiauthor anthology of gay writing in Southeast Asia and a finalist for the Lambda Literary Award in the US. His body of literary work is cited in *The Oxford Research Encyclopedia of Literature*, *The Princeton Encyclopedia of Poetry and Poetics* and *The Routledge Encyclopedia of Postcolonial Literature*. He has been a literature fellow at the Cambridge University Summer Seminar on

Contemporary Literature, the Bread Loaf Writers' Conference in Vermont, USA and most recently, the MacDowell Arts Residency in New Hampshire, USA. He is now writing his third novel set in New York City as well as his fourth collection of poems. He divides his time between Los Angeles and Southeast Asia.

OTHER BOOKS BY DANTON REMOTO

The Preying Birds (Mga Ibong Mandaragit), Penguin Random
House SEA, 2022
Banaag at Sikat (Radiance and Sunrise), Penguin Random
House SEA, 2021
Riverrun, A Novel, Penguin Random House SEA, 2020

ADVANCE PRAISE FOR *THE HEART OF SUMMER*

'Lush, limpid and lean, Danton Remoto is a stylist of the English language. Read him.'
—Bernice Rubens, winner of the Man Booker Prize
for the novel, *The Elected Member*

'I am a fan of the works of Danton Remoto.'
—Junot Diaz, winner of the Pulitzer Prize
and the National Book Critics' Circle Prize
for the novel, *The Brief Wondrous Life of Oscar Wao*

'Danton Remoto is an accomplished writer whose fiction is marked by elegant and intense language. I am also impressed by the social concern in his works, wrought well in images so clear it is like seeing pebbles at the bottom of a pond.'
—Sir Stephen Spender, Winner of the
Golden PEN Award, United Kingdom;
Poet Laureate of the United States

'Danton Remoto is a pioneer of gay writing in Southeast Asia. He writes poetry, fiction and non-fiction; his writing sparkles.'
—Paul Bailey, shortlisted for the Man Booker Prize
for the novels, *Gabriel's Lament* and
Peter Smart's Confessions

'Danton Remoto's books are vivid, well-written and enthralling. He is an adroit writer: his works form part of Asia's new heart.'
—James Hamilton-Paterson, Winner of the
Whitbread Prize for the novel, *Gerontius*

'Danton Remoto is one of the Philippines' best writers.'
—*The Age*, Melbourne

'Danton Remoto can capture curves of feeling and shapes of thought in his writings. His language is chiselled and lapidary, musical in its control and tonality. His eye and ear are perfect.'
—Professor Rolando S. Tinio, National Artist for
Literature and Theatre, Philippines;
British Council Scholar at the
University of Bristol

'When Danton Remoto joined the worlds of radio and television, I began to tease him as looking like a studious film star. He did appear in *Boy*, a controversial and prize-winning film by Aureaus Solito, where he played a difficult role—a poet and a creative writing teacher! But don't let that cheerful face deceive you: he is one of our most exquisite writers. His structure is impeccable, his language is lyrical, and his heart—especially his heart—is in the right place.'
—Gilda Cordero-Fernando, Awardee for
Literature and Publishing, Cultural Centre
of the Philippines; Author of *The Butcher, The Baker,
The Candlestick Maker* and *A Wilderness of Sweets and Other Stories*

'Danton Remoto is a professor of English, a prize-winning writer, and a veteran journalist. He is one of the best chroniclers of the contemporary scene in Asia.'
—*People Asia* Magazine

'How lucky we are to have the multi-genre writer Danton Remoto in one dazzling collection: the elegant and compassionate poet, the socio-politically charged journalist and the captivating storyteller who, like a witty and sensual Scheherazade, spins one remarkable story after another.'
—R. Zamora Linmark, Author of the novels,
The Importance of Being Wilde at Heart
and *Rolling the Rs*

'The Ateneo de Manila University has produced some of the finest Filipino writers in the last three decades. One of them is Danton Remoto, who writes poetry and prose of the highest order.'

—*Manila Chronicle*

'Danton Remoto is a gifted writer. His works have a contemporary flavour, dealing with topics that show delicately but thoroughly the Filipino heart.'

—*Philippine Daily Inquirer*

'The poetry and fiction of Danton Remoto are a sight to behold. He is raising a body of work that will be vital and enduring.'

—*The Evening Paper*

'Danton Remoto is the child of modern Asian literature in English. He studied well the American and British literary canons, and then he used that excellent training to write his own stories in a strange and beautiful English.'

—Father Joseph A. Galdon, S.J.,
World Literature Today

'Danton Remoto is a novelist with the heart of a poet.'

—Dr Edith Lopez Tiempo, National Artist of
Literature, Philippines; Fellow at the
Iowa Writers' Workshop under Robert Penn Warren

'The writings of Danton Remoto are like the quick strokes of calligraphy. The meanings are found not just in the words but also in the spaces, the silences within.'

—Edwin Morgan, OBE, Winner,
Queen Elizabeth's Gold Medal for Poetry;
Lifetime Achievement Award, Scottish Literary Arts Council

'Danton Remoto is a noted poet, fiction writer and newspaper columnist whose books have reached a wide audience in the Philippines and in Southeast Asia. Self-affirmation is highlighted in many of his writings.'
—*Routledge International Encyclopedia of Literature*

The Heart of Summer:
Stories and Tales

Danton Remoto

PENGUIN BOOKS

An imprint of Penguin Random House

PENGUIN BOOKS

USA | Canada | UK | Ireland | Australia
New Zealand | India | South Africa | China | Southeast Asia

Penguin Books is part of the Penguin Random House group of companies
whose addresses can be found at global.penguinrandomhouse.com

Published by Penguin Random House SEA Pvt. Ltd
9, Changi South Street 3, Level 08-01,
Singapore 486361

First published in Penguin Books by Penguin Random House SEA 2023

Copyright © Danton Remoto 2023

ISBN 9789815058178

Typeset in Garamond by MAP Systems, Bangalore, India

www.penguin.sg

*This book is dedicated to the blazing memories
of Gilda Cordero-Fernando, Nick Joaquin,
Kerima Polotan and Bienvenido N. Santos,
the amazing storytellers of the Philippines*

'Never say you know the last word about any human heart.'

—Henry James

'Through the years, a man peoples a space with
images of provinces, kingdoms, mountains, bays, ships
islands, fishes, rooms, tools, stars, horses and people.
Shortly before his death, he discovers that the patient
labyrinth of lines traces the image of his own face.'

—Jorge Luis Borges

'Time passes.'

—Ninotchka Rosca

Contents

THE SOUND OF THE SEA

This story is for my nieces and nephews

His father told Cody, 'This is the last time you'll see the ocean in our country.' They were walking on the sand in Boracay. Cody noticed the sand grains beginning to cling to his toes. He looked up. The sun was already high above the coconut trees, brilliant in the white canvas of the sky. His ears were filled with the sound of the waves, now rising, then crashing, on the shore. The water, he thought, was as blue as his mother's ceramic bowl at home.

Cody nodded, then asked: 'Dad, can I pick up the shells over there?'

'Of course, you may,' his father answered. He only reached up to his father's brown leather belt. The older man mussed up his hair, then added: 'I'll tell your sisters to join you later, okay?'

'Okay!' he said, 'I'll teach them how to make sandcastles.'

'Just don't go near the water yet. We will swim later. Your mom and I will join you.'

Cody smiled. Then he walked away from his father. The sand was beginning to burn. He thought it looked like the white soap detergent at home. He continued to walk, shielding his eyes with his palm to avoid the glare of the sun. He saw a small cowrie shell with dots of pink on its belly. He put it in the pocket of his shorts. Then he walked on and saw another shell: a brown one as smooth and polished as his skin.

The sound of the sea filled his ears. Cody walked on and picked up another shell with rib-like formations on its side. It was a violet shell. He even picked up the fragments of shells: white as paper, like torn wings. They're still shells, he thought, even if they're now broken.

He walked on and on. Then he saw a bivalve shell, as yellow as the sun; an orange shell shaped like his grandmother's wide-opened fan; and another blue shell smaller than his fingernail. One or more broken shells, and then finally, he had twelve shells. For the twelve months of the year, he thought, and then he smiled. Feeling content, he headed back to where he began.

Nicole, his older sister, and Alyssa, the one younger than him, were already running toward Cody.

Nicole was tall and clumsy, and she wore glasses. Alyssa when she smiled was brilliant.

Cody's eyes were as large and round as marbles. They brightened when he saw his sisters. He held their hands, and they sat down on the sand.

'Let's make sandcastles now,' said Nicole.

'I'll teach you how,' answered Cody.

'But I already know how!' Nicole shot back.

'Okay, I'll just teach Alyssa then.'

'*Ate* Nicole,' Alyssa asked, 'are we going to see sandcastles in America?'

'Only in Disneyland, if we visit Uncle Basil,' answered Nicole. Then she turned her back and began making her sandcastle.

Cody sat behind Alyssa. He put his palms behind the palms of his younger sister, then pushed her palms together, gathering sand and forming a small mound.

'This will be the wall,' he said as he patted the sand.

Alyssa screamed with glee.

'And this is the tower,' he added, as a column of sand rose before them. 'This is our window, and this is our door. Now, all we need is a flag.'

Alyssa's small eyes were filled with so much light. She smiled, revealing her baby teeth, which were white as milk.

'I'm done, too,' said Nicole, showing them her tall and thin castle.

'Yes! Yes!' chorused the girls.

Then, Cody dipped his hand into his pocket and put the shells slowly on the sand. He got the small cowrie shell with dots of pink on its belly. Then the brown one that was smooth and polished as his skin. The violet shell with rib-like formations on its side came next. And one by one, he put them gently on the sand.

The bivalve shell that was yellow as the sun.

The orange shell shaped like his grandmother's wide-open fan.

The blue shell that was smaller than his fingernail.

Then he also laid the broken shells on the sand.

'*Kuya* Cody,' Alyssa broke the silence, 'can I have one or two of these shells?'

'Okay,' Cody said, giving her the small cowrie shell with dots of pink on its belly. He also gave his sister the bivalve shell as yellow as the sun, because it reminded him of her brilliant smile.

'Umm, Cody, umm, your sandcastle is really nice,' Nicole began.

'I know,' Cody smiled, then waited.

'Can I also have some shells?'

He gave Nicole the violet shell with rib-like formations on its side. He also gave her the brown shell that was as smooth and polished as his skin.

'Thanks, Cody,' Nicole said, smiling brightly and wriggling her head.

'Now, I get to keep these,' he said, picking up the blue shell that was smaller than his fingernail. He laid it down on the sand, and then he picked up another shell: the orange one shaped like his grandmother's wide-open fan which she used during summer. He thought: I will put this orange shell on my windowsill in America, and this will always remind me of my grandmother back in the Philippines.

He also scooped up the six broken shells. Then he held them gently in the cup of his hand.

But then something happened. They first heard rather than saw it: the roar of a big wave. When they looked to their left, it was already coming—a blue wave topped with white froth, surging towards them. It rose and fell about them swiftly, suddenly. The children lost their balance and fell on the sand, cold and screaming.

But the wave just returned to the sea as quickly as it had come.

The seawater stung Cody's eyes. Through the mist of tears, he saw that their two sandcastles had crumbled. And the shells, too, were gone, claimed back by the sea. His sisters also saw what had happened, and they began to cry.

But Cody brushed the sand from his knee. Then, he stood up and held his sisters' hands. His two sisters also stood up, and he said, 'They're lost now, but we can go and find other shells. We've got time to pick them before Dad calls for us.'

So, the three young children walked again, their toes touching the white sand. They bent down to pick up a beautiful shell here, a broken one there—all gifts from the sea to remind them of their last summer in the old country.

BEGINNING

She pulled out her ballpen and pressed down a period, making a small hole on the last page of her blue exam book. The veins in her fingers seemed to twitch, the blue-green veins that looked like a mountain stream. She closed her blue exam book and sighed. After replacing the ballpen's cap, she walked to where the literature teacher stood and submitted her book without saying anything.

At last, she thought, as she walked out of the room, the second semester's over. The next two months loomed large in her mind, and she didn't even know yet how to begin her vacation! She knew she would not stay home all those two months. She rushed out of Berchman's Building towards the bus stop with the same energy she summoned at the sight of their family's brown, steel gate after completing her weekend jogging around the subdivision. Beyond the trees whose leaves whorled like green ink, the afternoon sky was already on fire.

* * *

'They have already left,' smiled Berta, the housemaid. Her dark skin glowed beneath the crystal-ball lanterns atop the concrete posts standing like sentinels on the gate.

'Why didn't they wait for me?' she asked, then left Berta without even waiting for an answer. She slumped down on the blue sofa and turned on the record player. Rod Stewart's songs rocked the living room.

'Ruby's graduation is at 7.30 p.m., and they waited for you until 6.30 p.m.,' said Berta, then turned away and went to the kitchen to reheat the food for dinner.

She stood up and walked to her room, feeling cheated. She thought, I'm going to miss the fun and the food at the celebration that will surely follow—and eat Berta's greasy food again. She changed into a loose shirt and sat on her bed, contemplating the wide, white square of the ceiling.

After dinner of fried fish and stewed mung bean with bitter-gourd leaves, she turned off the record player and turned on the television. The white dot grew larger until the outlines of people appeared. The evening news was still on, anchored by a beautiful woman she thought would be better off on a fashion ramp. But her delicate cheekbones, she thought further, thin-bridged nose, and small lips somewhat blurred the gore and violence of the news she was reading. The news, she thought, doesn't change. Just the names and places do.

'Margie,' cut in Berta.

She turned around. Berta had on her pink, cotton blouse, the one printed with miniature flowers, and blue denims. 'Where are you going?'

'I'm leaving tonight. Sir said you may sleep in your grandmother's room until they arrive.'

'Not now!' she exclaimed, surprised at the tremor in her voice. She snapped back the knob and saw the newscaster's beautiful features reduced to a white dot, and then, darkness.

'I'll go to my sister's house in Libis tonight,' Berta continued. 'The boat leaves for Iloilo at 10 p.m. The town fiesta will be on Saturday. Of course, I don't want to miss it—and the dancing as well.' She said all this, smiling a little. Then, she walked back to the maid's quarters.

So, everybody is now on vacation mode! she thought. She grabbed the glossy magazine and leaned back against the sofa. She flipped the pages, thinking: I have to stay home this summer and do the dishes and scrub the floor and take care of grandmother because Ma and Pa allowed Berta to leave without finding a replacement?

'Bye-bye, Margie,' Berta said. Margie stood up, following Berta who was carrying an old brown suitcase in one hand and a large can of biscuits in the other. Margie forced a dry smile and opened the gate.

'Happy trip, Berta,' she finally said, then closed the gate. The sound of the latch grated against her ears, reminding her of her grandmother who pushed the doorbell endlessly until somebody rushed out of the house to open the gate and carry her coming-home gifts, all of which were for Ruby.

'Here, take this *tocino*,' the old woman would say during breakfast, forking the meatiest cut of the sweet pork meat over to Ruby's plate. In the living room, the old woman shelled peanuts and watermelon seeds, giving them all to Ruby, who had an uncanny resemblance to the old woman's younger self.

'Don't mind your lola,' her father would often remind Margie, when he noticed Margie's lips had become more pouty than usual. 'She loves you too.'

Margie would just nod. But she did not understand why it was only Ruby whom the old woman brought home to Albay, who drank the goat's milk, who ate the summer fruits from the trees in the backyard of their grandmother's large, ancient house.

She closed the screen door, turned off the lights in the yard and walked to the guest room occupied by her grandmother. She turned the knob and pushed the door, which creaked a little.

There was a long bed with pink bedsheets; its wooden headboard had Mr and Mrs carved on it—the old bed of Margie's parents. In a corner of the bedroom was a shelf filled with

Ruby's grade-school books, arranged according to thickness. Beside the bed stood the upright piano, moved into the room because it no longer worked and only cluttered the living room. And in the centre of the room, the old woman slept on her bed.

Slowly, the old woman inclined her head to one side. Sentient still, Margie thought. The hooked nose, shaped like a parrot's beak, was the only remarkable feature in a face now riven with lines. The old woman's fingers moved to the commode beside her bed, groping for the horn-rimmed eyeglasses which she fitted over her ears. Then, she raised her wrinkled hand, loose with withered flesh, as if wanting to touch Margie. Margie walked towards her grandmother and cupped the hand that had the texture of parchment. Then, she brushed the old woman's hand against her forehead. 'Marga—Rita, *kumusta*? How are you?' the old woman said, her words floating in the room.

Margie nodded, and then sat in the old woman's rocking chair. She said, flatly, 'Lola, the final tests are over. I think I passed.' The chair rocked to and fro, reminding her of the white-capped waves seen from the beach in Oas, her grandmother's old hometown— Oas, a sleepy town between the green hills and the blue sea.

'Eight more years,' the old woman continued, gazing at the space between her and the high ceiling, 'before Ruby . . . becomes a doctor. She is the high-school valedictorian. I wish . . . I could have gone to her graduation tonight . . .' Her rheumy eyes seemed to light up. 'She can cure me,' she said with certainty. 'When I was teaching in Albay,' the old woman continued, 'the final tests were also difficult. I made sure they were difficult . . . hrrmmm.'

But the old woman began to cough. Her coughing, which was usually in short bouts, continued. Margie rose from her seat and opened the medicine cabinet near the door. She grabbed the cough syrup. The swell of coughing sounds rose, choking the room.

Margie supported the old woman's bony back and slowly helped her to sit upright. The old woman parted her dry lips as

Margie tilted the bottle, and the sticky syrup settled on the bottom of the teaspoon. Gently, she shoved it into her grandmother's mouth. Barely had she withdrawn the teaspoon, however, when the coughing continued again. The leathery face of her grandmother seemed to crumble with each spasm, her body bending into a painful arc. Margie wiped away the cold sweat on the old woman's brow, thinking: God, nobody's here except me. Before her eyes, the floors seemed to slant up to the ceiling. Her heart pounded.

She put down the teaspoon on the commode. 'Lola, Ruby will be here soon; Mama and Papa will be here soon as well,' she whispered. 'Everything's going to be all right.' But the coughing broke out again, louder and more insistent this time. She touched her grandmother's scrawny back, her fingers feeling the spine straining against the skin. Her grandmother used to stand up as straight as a ruler, but now her back was bent in the shape of the letter *C*. Margie shut her eyes and hugged her grandmother. But the coughing continued. A strange heat surged through the nose of Margie, rising to her eyes, remaining there.

After what seemed like many minutes, the coughing stopped. Quickly, Margie fluffed the pink pillows and gently rested her grandmother's head on it. The old woman's chest rose and fell slowly; her nose had turned a hint of red. After what seemed like a long time, sleep finally descended on her.

Margie kissed the wrinkled forehead, noting how the white hair now seemed like a veil around her grandmother's head, the same veil she had used to cover her head when she went to Mass every Sunday. Margie tiptoed out of the room, quietly closed the door, and then ran out upon hearing the honking of their car.

The stifling heat was gone now. A coolness seeped down from the night sky that was sown with stars. She opened the high, steel gate. Inside the car, she could see her father, mother and sister, aglow in the dark. Now, she thought as she stepped aside to let the car in, I have properly begun my summer vacation.

THE CHAMELEON YEARS

. . . These are
Chameleon years; windows change
Eyes. Doors alter ears.

—Alfred Yuson

Cesar stood in front of a house with a brown, steel gate. It had lichen-covered stone walls, with shards of glass embedded on top of the walls. He hesitated for a moment, but he finally pressed the button. A low, buzzing sound shattered the silence. He heard the sound of slippers moving toward the gate. The shuffling of feet stopped on the other side.

'*Tiyang*, this is Cesar,' he said, and now he heard the latch being lifted. Surely, it could not be his aunt who now stood before him. He looked at the white, silk-smooth hair secured in a bun and the cracked lines on her face. His eyes darted to her neck, and there was the big, black mole near her collar bone. It was reassuring, this familiar mole on her neck, for he had not gone to their house in Albay for many years.

'Tiyang Onda,' he said in the singsong lilt of Oasnon, at the same time bending a little and bringing her hand to his lips. As he raised his face, she broke into a smile. Her teeth were stained with nicotine from the long, black Bataan cigarettes that she smoked, the lighted end often hidden inside her mouth, even when she was in the city.

'O, 'Sar, how was your trip? Come inside,' she said.

'The train was fast this time,' he answered as he walked in, his eyes scanning the yard of the house where he had lived during his high-school and college years. The light-blue paint of the house was beginning to flake off. His aunt shut the gate. In the yard, the Bermuda grass was already fat and thick in places. At its edges, the hibiscus plants were already heavy with flowers—red, yellow and orange blossoms, their petals faintly astir in the breeze of this December morning.

'I think you always spend your afternoons here,' he said, indicating the yard, 'weeding the lawn so they won't overrun the Bermuda grasses.' He noticed the bingo wings on her arms.

'That's true,' she replied as she stamped her feet on the coloured mat by the doorstep, outlining the word 'Welcome'. 'You sit here on the sofa while I get *ginàtan* for you. There's more than enough for Mary and me.'

'Where's Mary?' he asked, in his mind seeing a large-eyed girl in ponytails, his aunt's youngest daughter.

'She's still in school. She is now in fourth year high school and taller than me!' she replied, smiling at the memory of her daughter, before disappearing into the kitchen.

He put down his black briefcase on the floor. His eyes fell on a photo album above the wooden table to his right. He had vague memories of this photo album. The years, aah, the years had a way of making even the most indelible images fade. They had come to the city because his father wanted him to study at the University of the Philippines, the old man's alma mater. They rented an apartment in Project 4, Quezon City, and later bought a house on a lot in one of the new subdivisions in Antipolo, now that a new highway had opened up between the bustling towns of Marikina and Cainta. His father intended for them all to stay in the city forever. 'Everything is here, my son,' his father would say while they travelled on the highway. Both sides of the highway used to be rice fields, miles and miles of rice fields, with the grains turning ripe every May and November.

He picked up the photo album and opened its green cover. He flipped through the pages indifferently, looking at the images of his high-school friends and himself, wondering how those lanky figures that almost looked like sticks could gain weight in just a few years. He looked at his watch: I still have an hour to spare, he told himself. He continued leafing through the album, chuckling at how clumsy they had been when they were younger, until he saw the photograph of Mrs Medina and her family towards the end of the album. The smile on her face seemed to jump out to the world outside the white borders of the photograph. His throat tightened. Mrs Medina had been his music teacher in his first year.

As he looked more closely at the photograph, at Mrs Medina's parted lips, he now thought that his teacher had been laughing when the camera clicked. It was taken the morning after her first day in Saint Louis, Missouri, in front of her sister's house, as her handwriting at the back indicated. It was a family portrait. Captain Medina grinning from ear to ear (like a Cheshire cat, or so he thinks), his right arm draped around the shoulders of Mrs Medina, with their three young children lined up in front of them. In the background stood a big apple tree, the red fruits peeking through the green translucence of leaves.

It had been Cesar's first day in high school in the city, and he wished he was still in the province. After his classes in Oas, he and the boys in the neighbourhood would fly their kites in the wind or swim in the clean and cold river. But that day, many miles away from their ancient house in Albay, he sat on a cold, concrete bench, staring at the mimeographed sheet of paper outlining his class schedule. He tightened his grip on his spiral notebooks, newly covered with plastic, as if wanting to squeeze something from them.

His first class was from 10.30 to 11.30 in the morning. The music room was already half-filled with his new classmates. The searching looks of strangers were directed at him as he entered the classroom. It seemed as if their penetrating eyes flicked over him, stripping him to the bone. He walked to the front row and sat on the chair. The bell rang harshly, and through the door rushed a big-boned woman. She was carrying an umbrella. She put her things on the table, her eyes scanning the room.

She said, 'Sorry for coming in like this. I thought I'd be late for our first meeting.' The fat quivered around her lips as she spoke, enunciating the words through fine, even teeth. Her wide-set eyes smiled along with her mouth. She turned around and picked up a piece of chalk. She wrote her name on the board.

'I'm Mrs Lina Medina, your music teacher and homeroom adviser,' she told them. She looked tough, but something inside told him he would enjoy her class.

It was two weeks later when she informed the class that Cesar would be the class beadle. He shook his head, disagreeing vehemently, so she said nothing more about it. He sighed with relief and believed she had already forgotten about it. The day was hot, unusual for June and July, with the tropical cyclones cutting through the country, howling like banshees. But that day, there were only the heat waves that seemed to burn his skin. The thought of an added burden on his schedule annoyed him. After the class, he quickly made his way to the door, but then, Mrs Medina came over and gently tapped him on the shoulder.

'Cesar, why don't you want to be the class beadle?' she asked. 'You're the right fit for it. You sit in front and your other teachers told me that you always arrive early in class.' She had a cool and calm voice. There was something in her that vaguely reminded him of his mother.

He fumbled for words. 'I sit in front because my eyes are bad, and I come early to class because I live near the school,' he answered, avoiding her gaze that was fixed on his face. He knew the answers were too pat, but he did not care. And then he added, releasing the words so fast they tumbled over each other: 'Besides, I don't know my classmates. They might laugh at my voice, which always breaks.'

He winced a little, for his finger had finally found the source of his restlessness; that, along with the sparse moustache on his upper lip and the pimples on his face, had made him feel like a strange new creature. He also could not understand his strange moods, the ache to be alone at times, in a room full of silence. And now, this new school in a noisy city that seemed to be hemmed in by walls.

Mrs Medina broke the silence. 'If you're the beadle, you'll know them all in a week's time. Besides, those things you mentioned are just natural for teenagers. Your classmates also have them.' Her diphthongs rose and fell musically as she talked.

'Okay,' he said, his voice full and loud. 'I'll be the beadle.' As he spoke, he felt that trusting child in him returning, flying a kite in the wind or swimming in the river.

He swiftly settled into his new role as the days passed. He checked the attendance and collected the National Red Cross contributions. He divided the class into five groups and assigned to them the topics outlined in the homeroom kit that Mrs Medina had given to him. The groups presented songs, dances, skits and pantomimes to bring to life their topics which ranged from 'How to Make Friends' to 'Study Tips and Techniques'. The class would sometimes tease Mrs Medina, because when it finally rained, she opened her umbrella inside the class. There were holes on the galvanized-iron roof and the rain fell right down on her teacher's table.

He was grateful for the responsibility, because it kept him too busy to worry about himself all the time.

Gradually, his sense of aloneness vanished as he became aware that his classmates and he were just boys and girls growing up, with the same fears and dreams. Their pimples didn't turn into warts, the boys' voices broke because they would later deepen, and the girls, their legs seemed to grow longer.

He was amazed at how quickly everything could change and told himself that he would be a teacher, a fine teacher like Mrs Medina. The school year was almost over when Mrs Medina left with her three children to join her husband in the United States. Her husband worked with the US Navy. On Recognition Day, his father pinned on him a gold medal for being the First Honours awardee in his first-year class. He was swamped with flash bulbs and hands eager to congratulate him, garlands of jasmines hung around his neck, but he was sad because Mrs Medina was leaving.

She walked over to him as he descended the stone stairs, and she congratulated him. 'My best student. Not just this year, but in my many, many years of teaching.' He smiled and felt like he had grown taller. When he looked at her face, he saw her smile as well. However, it was a sad smile.

The Christmas that followed was memorable for him, because Mrs Medina sent him a photograph along with a clothbound book that arrived on the morning of December 23. The book contained the tales spun by Scheherazade for a thousand and one nights. He spent the whole day reading the book, thumbing through its crisp pages, inhaling the strange, sweet smell of its newness, trying to read all the fantastic stories in one sitting until his eyes nearly popped out of their sockets.

* * *

It was April, and he was graduating with a literature degree from the State University the following week. The sunflowers were all abloom on University Avenue, nodding their golden heads at everyone. And the clear blue sky seemed to stretch into infinity.

He had just finished packing his college books and notes in brown, milk cartons. After eight years in the city, his father wanted to return home to Albay. Cesar would go back home with them.

Unlike his classmates from the State University, Cesar did not take his graduate studies in the United States or join an advertising office at the central business district in Makati, which seemed the fashionable thing to do. He had decided to teach, inspired as he was by Mrs Medina. And he planned to do this in his elementary school in the province, his former school where he first learnt to read and write. His old school nestled on the toenail of a hill was like a womb, giving him security and warmth.

A deep joy filled his heart. At last, they were going home; home to the place where he was born. He wondered at the swift passage of the years, as if they had wings. Suddenly, the button on the gate rang. He started and fumbled for his flip-flops on the floor. He half ran outside and quickly opened the brown, steel gate. In front of him was a messenger seated on his motorcycle, thrusting a telegram at him. He took it and signed a piece of paper to acknowledge receipt. The messenger started the machine and sped off, leaving him wondering whether the telegram came from the principal of his elementary school in the province, replying to an enquiry he had made for a teaching position there. Slowly, he opened the telegram that was wrapped in red plastic. Something trembled in him as the words sprang out at him. It said that Mrs Medina was back from the States, but she was paralysed. The message came from Captain Medina. Cesar just stood in the yard, hearing nothing, but he felt as if a wall was closing in.

He stood as if rooted, until he heard the familiar roar of their car's engine, followed by the horn honking. He opened the gate and looked at his parents in their blue Volkswagen. It was already getting dark and as he looked up at the sky, he saw it splashed with red and orange. He told his parents the news. They told him they would visit Mrs Medina. He ran back to the house to change and came back in an instant. They drove to Marikina, to the house of Mrs Medina.

Night already covered the mountains of Antipolo as his father drove down the new highway. The rice fields were gone, paved over with concrete and replaced now by subdivisions, where houses were being built in a frenetic fashion even at night.

The car turned left from Juan Sumulong Highway and entered a subdivision. The mountain wind sent a chill through Cesar's body as he stepped out of the car. Overhead arched the cloudless sky; the cold stars shone.

Captain Medina opened the gate and gave them a sad smile. 'The children went with my mother,' he said. He seemed to have aged quickly, the white hair growing on his temples. Their yard was redolent with the fragrance of *dama de noche,* the plant often called the lady of the night. The cicadas chorused their night calls. Captain Medina looked at Cesar and smiled his sad smile again.

'Exactly two days before her stroke, she asked me what gift she could send you for your graduation from the university. That was last December.'

He remembered his last letter to them had been sent in the third week of November. When no reply came to his letter, he had felt bad but had told himself that she might not have received the letter yet.

'She had an argument with her niece who lives with us,' the captain recounted. 'Claire's American father had divorced Lina's sister. She left her daughter with us. Claire's been coming home late and Lina, worried about what she was into, confronted Claire one night; no, it was already one in the morning when Claire came home. Lina became so fired up that her blood pressure rose. Then she had the stroke.'

Cesar found himself wondering what had happened to the patience his teacher had shown them many years ago. They entered the bungalow, its interior well lighted, with a tapestry of

The Last Supper hung in front of the dining table. There was a piano in the corner, with a white crocheted cover cascading down its sides, like a waterfall. He sat down on a blue sofa whose cushions sank under him.

'She stayed three months in the hospital,' Captain Medina said. 'I asked the doctor to save her, whatever the cost . . .' and then, his voice quivered, 'but she is now paralysed. She can't speak any more.'

Cesar was just quiet, but he felt a pulse had quickened in his temple.

Captain Medina cleared his throat and resumed, 'We arrived four days ago, but I had to have us settled first before I could wire you. We don't have a telephone connection here, so I wasn't able to ring you up. I know you're one of the first people she would have wanted to see, even now . . . in her condition.'

'How long will you stay here?' Cesar's mother broke in.

'Oh, about a month,' he said. 'Here we have relatives who can take care of Lina, while I'm away aboard my ship.'

The housemaid appeared with soft drinks and cookies on a silver tray.

'I hope the children won't take it too hard,' my father said, as she put the frosted glasses on the mahogany table the colour of old wine.

'Do you want to see her now?' Captain Medina asked Cesar after he ate several cookies. He lifted his face and looked at the older man.

'Yes,' Cesar said, surprised at the evenness of his voice. They all stood up and walked to the other room. He walked after his mother who followed the two men.

Mrs Medina was already sleeping when they entered the room. A thin white blanket covered her up to her chest. They sat on the chairs near her bed. She was in a white housedress, looking more like an apparition than a real person. She stirred from her sleep and opened her eyes. They looked different now, with a yellowish membrane girding the grey pupils that used to be black. He wondered whether he saw a glimmer of laughter sparkle in her eyes. But, upon looking again, there was only a blank, uncomprehending stare. There was no more fat under her chin.

'Ma'am,' he said as he moved up and sat on the edge of the bed.

'She can't speak,' Captain Medina reminded him gently.

He knew he would do anything just to make her speak again. The body that used to have so much energy was stiff. She was, indeed, paralysed from the neck down. No words issued from her lips, not even a whimper or a whisper.

After a long time, they left. As they walked towards the gate, he felt as though his shoulders had been cast in cement. Overwhelmed by the sadness in the spaces around them, the cicadas had ceased their blithe chirping in the darkness.

* * *

But now, the sunlight streamed from the open jalousies of the window on this other morning, forming a small pool of brightness beneath his feet. He put the spoon back into the bowl of ginàtan that he had just eaten, delighted with the sticky sweetness of the plantain and sago balls cooked in coconut milk. Then, he thought that he had not seen his teacher for a long time. Ten years, in fact. Mrs Medina had died two months after their visit. They all went to her wake, an occasion that filled him with such sadness. Her children and husband had returned to the States a year after her death.

He abruptly closed the photo album. Its cardboard covers shut with a hollow thud. He returned it to the metal shelf.

'Mary loves to look at that album and giggle at your looks when you were in high school,' Tiyang Onda said as she sat on the wooden-backed chair in front of him.

'Tiyang,' he said, and stopped suddenly, not wanting to continue what he would say. 'Father . . . father says our grocery in the province isn't doing well.'

'Yes, I noticed the last time I went home that there's a new supermarket in the town centre.'

'Father said he's going to accept Mr Yu's offer to buy this house and lot,' he said, with a rush of breath, adding, 'Mr Yu plans to build a petrol station here.'

She was quiet for a while, her lips parted in surprise. His aunt had been living in this house for ten years, as a caretaker, when they all left for the city. Then she said, 'I see. This corner lot will fetch a high price.' Her voice was strangely soft and, he noted, carried no trace of bitterness. Or was she just suppressing her emotions, the way it was done in this country? Shielding her sadness with a façade of steely strength?

When Cesar spoke again, the words came out in a rush, a cascade he did not want to stop, for fear he would not be able to accomplish his mission.

'Father needs the money to buy a house and lot in Naga City. That city is now booming, unlike our hometown here. He told me that you and Mary can live with them. The house is big; there are several vacant rooms. I'm going to buy a condo unit near the advertising office in Makati that I'm joining this summer. I'm tired of teaching, Tiyang. You can take your time. You need not worry about the things to be brought to Naga City—just your clothes and the things you want to bring with you. The movers can just bring everything to Naga City in a big truck.'

'That is okay, Cesar. Mary can study at Colegio de Santa Isabel in Naga City. It's a good school. Anyway, the refrigerator is already old, and the television set isn't working. I think the only thing I can save is the gas range and oven.' She spoke calmly, but Cesar noted a glassy film cover her eyes.

Then, she picked up the empty bowl, turned her back, and went into the kitchen.

Left alone in the living room, he stood up and retrieved a book on the shelf. It was a clothbound book, the words *The Arabian Nights* on its cover smudged with a bit of dust. Slowly, he opened it and saw that some of its pages were already gone, eaten by silverfish. Two brown cockroaches' eggs had lodged themselves near the spine of the book. He flicked them off, but the brown stains remained. He pulled out the handkerchief from the back pocket of his trousers to wipe away the stains, but a thought suddenly came to him. It was so sudden that he immediately put down the book beside the tall pile of his high-school books.

The thought that had bothered him before was about how he would reach the office of Integrity Advertising Associates in Makati before 9 a.m. tomorrow so he could submit the documentation required for joining the company. A former classmate headed it, and he had offered him a starting salary of ten thousand pesos, more than triple the pittance he got from teaching grade VI students not to write 'I wanted to *drank* . . .' in their theme papers. He had also grown irritated by the dark moods of his students, these teenagers who had felt so entitled to so many things that they did not deserve.

He picked up his black briefcase and called to his aunt who was stirring the pot in the kitchen. She put down the ladle and smoothened her duster. He walked over to her and smiled sadly. He told her he would be back in a fortnight, with Mr Yu.

'I've a plane to catch in Legazpi City, Tiyang Onda. Have to rush now to the town centre to meet the driver who'll bring me to the airport.'

He walked to the gate where the vines of morning glory bloomed, with the purple trumpets of flowers reaching for the sun.

However, the thought of being late for his plane made him walk faster.

LOLA

This is for Nick Joaquin, our National Artist for Literature

It was the first day of class and the traffic was terrible. Wanda left the house at 6 a.m., her skin still tingling from her shower, cool in her loose, white shirt and black jeans. After an hour on a jeepney, she reached the university. She reeked of petrol fumes, her shirt showing creases and folds.

But her classmates! As usual, they paraded themselves in the lobby of the administration building in their crisp clothes, talking about *Miss Saigon* which they had watched at the West End in London, or about the beggars in the subways of New York. Wanda just walked past them, remembering her summer in Bataan—the sea unrolling itself before her, like a blue carpet; the air a distilled pureness—then began arranging her class cards by schedule, to be handed with a nervous smile to a new set of teachers.

If going out of the house was hard, coming home was hell. Just as she was flagging down a jeepney, the weak sunlight gave way to the rains of June, which fell like a thick, grey sheet, changing everything. The dust on the streets became mud and the potholes, puddles. With its plastic flaps down on its sides, the interior of the jeepney began to burn like a furnace. It filled with the smell of trapped air and the stink of afternoon sweat. Then the man from across her began to smoke. She feigned a cough. No effect. Two. Nothing. So, she just stared at him, hard.

Nada, nyet, non, wala talaga! The man had the hide of a rhinoceros. And so, smelling of other people's sweat and cigarette smoke, she got off at the corner before the jeepney rounded the bend leading to Hillside. Their house was located on a street fronting the elementary school, with its tall trees like sceptres against the sky. Nonetheless, they still felt lucky—the air that filled their lungs day in and day out was not as polluted as what other people had to endure in the First Lady's City of Man.

She pushed the white button on the brown gate and knew that the housemaid, Ludy, was already coming, merely from the sound of her slippers on the driveway. Ludy smiled (perhaps, her mother hadn't scolded the maid today). Then Wanda saw her.

Sitting on Wanda's favourite rocking chair, swaying to and fro, beside her mother's greenhouse of blooming pink orchids, was an old woman. Her profile stood out sharply against the grey granite walls of the house. Wanda was sure that her father's parents were long gone, and that her mother's relatives, with their green cards, were in chaotic and colourful Los Angeles. Must be another relative from Bataan. As if in answer to Wanda's unspoken question, Ludy gently patted the old woman's shoulders: 'Lola, this is Wanda, the eldest daughter of Sir and Ma'am.'

Hair, white like abaca fibres, framed her lined face. Her cheekbones were high, even noble-looking. Her eyes were swimming in rheum. She spoke in English, articulating her words very well indeed.

'Good afternoon, Wanda. I accompanied my grandson, Billy, to school today. I was waiting for him in front of the variety store on the street corner when it began to rain. Your father's car was passing by, and he asked me to wait here in your house,' she said, in her soft diphthongs.

Wanda smiled. Another gesture of kindness to strangers from my crazy father, she thought. Then she said, 'Why don't you wait inside, Lola? It's cooler there.'

Ludy made impatient gestures, criss-crossing her palms before her own eyes and shaking her head. Of course, I know she's blind, Wanda wanted to snap at Ludy; I'm not stupid, no? But the old woman had begun swinging the rocking chair again, slowly, silently . . .

Like the leaves of memory falling from the trees in the black wind, the old woman drifts into the past. She remembered her father, his skin brown as the rich volcanic loam in Albay. He had a square face, like a sheet of paper, on which were written the marks of the years: how he joined the Revolution against Spain at the age of fifteen—so small that the Spanish soldiers let him pass through their sentry posts, the messages from one zone to the other cunningly sewn into the hemlines of his *calzoncillos*, his knee-length shorts; and when the Revolution was won, how the new conquerors, the Americans, arrived, ostensibly as friends of the Philippine revolution. She still remembered her father railing against the new conquerors, how they 'bought' the Philippines for 20 million dollars from Spain that had already been defeated— and humiliated—by the natives from island to island.

'What a bargain,' her father had said with a bitter smile, chewing on his betel nut and spitting its red juice on the ground. 'With a population of 10 million, we were worth only $2 per head!' And so, with the help of the mayor, the bastard son of a Spanish friar and a local maiden, the Americans—their eyes as blue as the sky and their hair bleached golden in the tropical sun—occupied the town of Oas in the way they had occupied the other towns in the whole archipelago, save for the proud Muslim South. And the cavalry men hid their Krags and Mausers, still smoking from the bullets that had killed hundreds of thousands of Filipinos, changed into civilian clothes, put on the air of all-American boys who were tall and muscle-bound from all that fresh, cow's milk and hot apple pie, and began recruiting young Filipinos for school so they could learn the new language: English. It was like Ali Baba's secret word, they claimed, a talisman, this new language that would open the caves of darkness, revealing pearls and diamonds, silver and gold, rubies and emeralds, the sheer brilliance spilling over from the treasure chests of dark wood, down to the thick, soft magical carpets that could seemingly fly.

She remembered her mother, who had helped her father work in the rice fields after the Revolution when she was not fixing breakfast, lunch or dinner, or giving birth to any of her ten children. Her mother made the richest, most fragrant chocolate from the cocoa trees that grew in luxuriance in their backyard. When the rains would fall on their thatched nipa hut during the early mornings, leaving a chill that would settle over them like a cold breath, her mother would light a wick floating in a jar of coconut oil, pad into the kitchen (her bare feet soundless on the bamboo floor), pour water from the earthen jar into the kettle, drop the balls of cocoa into the kettle and bring the water to a boil, then later, hand each of them the tin white cups of steaming chocolate, which the children would pour on their tin white plates of glutinous rice that they always ate with their mother's special chocolate; then eat the dried fish, which her mother had fried to a crisp.

Her father did not want her to go to school.

'Guillerma, what will you learn from those Yanquis?' But her mother insisted that she had brains and, therefore, she should go to school. The ten children all went to school in morning and afternoon shifts, so there would always be somebody to draw water from the well or help transplant the rice saplings from their seedbeds into the fields.

Every day, they walked 5 kilometres to school and 5 kilometres back home. School was a clump of three thatched nipa huts, all slightly bigger than their house. Their teacher was only twenty years old: Private Thomas O'Donnell. He spoke the new language in a strangely musical way, reminding her of the way they spoke their Bikol in Albay, their diphthongs rising and falling gently like the slopes of the majestic Mayon Volcano, with its perfectly shaped cone. Private O'Donnell, or 'Tom', as he liked to be called, read from a thick, hardbound book, whose crisp, fragrant pages spoke of John and Judy and their dog, Spot; children with white skin and blond hair, like their teacher, all cheerful and filled with a sense of purpose, thanking the stars and God with a large roasted turkey on Thanksgiving Day.

In the days and months that followed, she learnt the alphabet: '*A* as in apple, *B* as in basketball, *C* as in cherry pie.' They read from the handbills and posters plastered on the walls of the municipal hall that the Filipino generals still fighting in the hills were not really generals but '*bandidos y ladrones*', bandits and thieves, as proven by their scandalously long hair and their inability to grasp the idea of what the posters called 'America's Benevolent Assimilation'. Her teacher spoke of a big old man garbed in red called Santa Claus who leaves his house in the North Pole, travels all over the world on a sled pulled by a herd of reindeer led by the red-nosed Rudolph, then slides down the chimney every Christmas Eve to deliver gifts to the obedient children. One day, she wondered, as she was walking home on the burning streets of Oas, the streets beginning to ripen with mats of yellow rice grains left to dry under the sun, how a blast of snow would feel against the skin, how it would feel to look outside the misted glass of the windowpane and see nothing, but a landscape of leafless trees and a cold whiteness enough to crack your bones.

Her teacher also taught them some songs, one of which she will never forget:

> *My bonnie lies over the ocean*
> *My bonnie lies over the sea*
> *My bonnie lies over the ocean*
> *Oh, bring back my bonnie to me.*

After teaching them this song, their teacher's blue-green eyes brimmed over with tears. She was embarrassed for him—her father had said that only women cry, so what did that make of Private O'Donnell? He apologized, saying that he had learnt that song from his parents when he was growing up, and in the air of the classroom floated words like 'potato famine' and 'the green, green grass of home' and 'Ireland'.

She did well in school. Her father had wanted only her brothers to go on to high school. But that meant studying in the next town.

'Expensive,' her father had said, clucking his tongue, chewing on his betel nut and spitting the red juice on the ground. 'Less labour in the fields.' But her mother had insisted that Guillerma—being the eldest in the family and being the class valedictorian of the Oas Elementary School, Class of 1925—should go on to high school in Ligao.

She did go on to high school, learning to parse the English language from the American teachers who came aboard the cattle ship, *U.S.S. Thomas*, thus the label 'Thomasites' stuck to these early American teachers. O, pioneers! The tall women wore ankle-length dresses and wide-brimmed hats, the men sweating in their grey suits, all of them fired by a sense of mission. She loved Henry Wadsworth Longfellow's 'Evangeline: A Tale of Arcadie', which follows an Arcadian girl named Evangeline and her search for her lost love, Gabriel, during the time of the Expulsion of the Arcadians. She rolled the rhythms of the poem on her tongue:

This is the forest primeval. The murmuring pines and the hemlocks,
Bearded with moss, and in garments green, indistinct in the twilight,
Stand like Druids of eld, with voices sad and prophetic,
Stand like harpers hoar, with beards that rest on their bosoms.
Loud from its rocky caverns, the deep-voiced neighbouring ocean
Speaks, and in accents disconsolate answers the wail of the forest . . .

She delighted in its evocations of loss of love and heartbreak and eventual hope, reciting it to herself as she walked home from school to the house of *Tia* Esmeralda, her aunt who lived three blocks away.

The Albay Normal School was offering scholarships for education majors, said the announcement on the bulletin board in front of the administration building. She squinted to make out the letters, because she had just come from the street outside, the sunlight blazing on her back, into the cool shadows of the school building. With the blessings of her parents and teachers, she took the train bound for Legazpi City to apply for the scholarship, which she got. And there, on the sprawling college campus, she met Alberto.

'Excuse me, but are you also in the normal school?' asked the man beside her. She looked at him—a dark-skinned, young man who was almost good-looking, trying to be witty on the first day of class.

She gave him a tight smile. Then: 'So are you.'

But he just smiled back, widely, with a chuckle, then said his name. She told him hers. He said, 'So you're Guillerma Regala? Your surname begins with the letter R, you must be from the town of Oas, then.'

'Yes,' she said, but their conversation was cut short when their teacher, Mr Dale, who had a particularly bad case of freckles on his arms and face, asked for their class cards. Despite herself (she only wanted to do well in school, become a teacher and then send her brothers and sisters to school), despite her Tia Esmeralda (who said that men are *tentacion*, the rotten apple of temptation that women should avoid at all costs), she began seeing Alberto after classes. He came from the town of Tabaco, the scion of a prominent Chinese-Filipino family with investments in the abaca trade. Every fortnight, ships sailed out of Tabaco's fine harbour, carrying hemp that would thereafter be known throughout the world as 'Manila Hemp' to the chagrin of the Bicolanos.

But Alberto had turned his back on the family business. 'Everybody in the family has dipped his finger in the pie. I want to be different. And teaching,' he would say, between mouthfuls of *maja blanca*, the white, glutinous rice cake and sips from his bottle of soda, 'teaching is for me; it is the most noble profession.' And Guillerma would agree with him about the nobility of their profession, something that Mr Dale had often reminded them.

But the stock-market crash of Wall Street in 1929 reverberated around the world, its aftershocks reaching even the town of Tabaco and its prosperous harbour. The Americans ordered smaller and smaller quantities of hemp that they turned into rope. The only ropes left in America, Alberto snorted, were quickly being snapped up by stockbrokers and assorted businessmen for their hangman's noose. The abaca industry came to a standstill. Hundreds of men were left without jobs. Alberto talked his family into giving separation pay to their workers. That—or as Alberto told her later, in a grave tone so unlike him—that, or the workers and their families, their children and their children's children, would spit on the graves of Alberto's family for generations on end. She wanted to tell Alberto, as they were walking out into the black asphalted street, the horse-drawn carriages clip-clopping before them, that the real reason, perhaps, was that Alberto didn't want a hungry mob to pry open the gates of their family's granary and cart away their sacks of *wagwag* and *milagrosa* rice, or worse, steal outright the money that his father was hoarding inside the hollows carved into the *narra* hardwood posts of their house. But these, she thought, are more real—and therefore, less romantic reasons—so she just kept quiet and let Alberto bask in the glow of his family's largesse.

Alberto and Guillerma finished college with honours.

She began teaching at the Oas Central Elementary School. The buildings were now made of wood and the floor of concrete, with the mother-of-pearl shells on the windows filtering the glare of the sun. Alberto taught in Camalig, a town that was 21 kilometres away. They kept up a lively correspondence that he addressed to her friend, Estrella, for her father forbade her from entertaining suitors.

'At the young age of twenty-three?' he would ask, puffing at his cigarette, the thin clouds of white smoke framing his face. She wanted to argue that he had married her mother when she was only fifteen (imagine, fifteen!). But you never, ever answer back. To do so would mean a sharp rebuke from him ('Is that what you learnt in school?'), or a stare from him that could burn you to a cinder, or when he was really roaring drunk and the fuse of his patience had burnt all the way down, he would slap her. Then would follow the silent and empty days, when a raw hurt would throb about the house, leaving everybody on edge. Since she did not want any of these dramas to happen to her (especially the last, at the age of twenty-three), she just held her peace.

Thus, she taught at the elementary school, and at the end of the month handed her pay to her father. Thirty pesos, quite a sum in the 1930s, the crisp bills inside the long, brown envelope, along with the list of things she needed: five pesos for a dress, two pesos for sundry. Every month, they would talk about 'sundry' ('You walk to school, so there's no expense for transportation; you eat your meals at home, so there are no expenses for food.'). She would have to spell it out to him patiently, point by point, that one needs some extra cash in the pocket for emergencies. But she thought everything was worth it. There was now enough food in the house. Her brothers and sisters were certainly going to school, their cheeks beginning to fill out with the Liberty condensed milk and the Star margarine that her mother could now afford to buy every week.

Seven long years of these: the walk from house to school, then back to the house again; the letters from Alberto, written in blue stationery, then folded into a thin blue envelope, which Estrella would wrap in a plastic sheet, hide at the bottom of her wicker basket filled with dried fish and vegetables and meat wrapped in several layers of newspaper (for she always passed by Guillerma's house after she had gone to the market) and hand over to her friend, a wicked smile playing on her lips; the twice-a-month dates with Alberto, on the pretext of a teachers' seminar, or an errand for the district supervisor . . .

Before a dessert of *halo-halo* in their favourite restaurant in Legazpi City, Alberto and Guillerma would talk about the days that had just passed, their students' enthusiasm (or lack of it), their families and friends, probing each other's feelings, while before them, the yellow beans, the thin fragrant slices of jackfruit (soft and smooth like skin), the transparent balls of sago, the crumbled custard, the chunks of sweet boiled bananas, the scoops of mango ice cream, everything swam in the sea of milk and crushed ice, and the tall glasses shivered, beads of sweat breaking out over their sides.

In the first week of December 1940, with the blessings of their families, finally, and at the age of thirty, Alberto and Guillerma were married. She remembered that day, like photographs that would never fade from her mind: her father uncomfortable in his crisp, new *barong tagalog*, the native wear made from spun pineapple fibres, escorting her gallantly to the altar, but you could see from his eyes a mixture of sadness and hesitation in giving her away to 'a complete stranger' (his own words); her mother beaming in her new dress, surrounded by her nine other grown-up children; the rain of rice grains, the explosion of light and white noise that greeted them as Alberto and Guillerma walked on the soft, red carpet towards the heavy baroque door of the ancient church in a solemn procession; the lavish spread prepared by the couple's countless relatives; the night they first made love in the room that Alberto grew up in, on the walls the photographs of young Alberto during his elementary-school graduation (pomaded hair, dutiful smile), Alberto as the captain of the basketball team in college (face glistening with sweat, muscles on those legs), how the years had changed him from child to boy to man, and now, to her lover, making her skin leap to life, loving her in the most tender manner . . .

After that came the war. Time's shutter clicked so swiftly, so mercilessly: Pearl Harbour, the Japanese Imperial Army landing in the Lingayen Gulf; Manila being declared an 'Open City'; her husband, her brothers, her father (who insisted he would go, 'I'm only fifty'), all of them joining the guerrillas in the hills to drive back the new conquerors, the daily humiliation of bowing deeply before the uncouth Japanese soldiers (with their garrulous language, their hobnailed boots, the long bayonets on the tips of their dangerous rifles); the difficulty of teaching with textbooks whose pictures, whose very words, had been drowned in a flood of black ink; the sense of danger rising out of her skin, so strong it would swamp the entire room, whenever Alberto—almost in rags, unshaven, his eyes tired and sad—would drop by for his sudden and secret visits.

And then, after three years of living on the edge, the so-called Liberation: American tanks rolling on the streets and planes shooting down the Japanese hiding in the walled city of Intramuros, the Americans bombing the grand old buildings, pounding the ancient churches with cannon balls, walls and roofs collapsing, erasing 400 years of history, leaving nothing else but the skeletal frames of buildings, bombed-out houses, a landscape of ruins.

Spam, G.I. babies, the jeepney. One administration after another: Manuel Roxas, who allowed American bases on the soil of a free country; Elpidio Quirino, whose ludicrous golden chamber pot, which was a gift, led to charges of corruption; Ramon Magsaysay Jr, the man of the masses and the so-called darling of the Free World; Carlos Garcia, who was so kind he did not see the pillage going on about him; Diosdado Macapagal, whose Land Reform Act got stuck in the mud of a country owned by only sixty greedy families; Ferdinand Marcos Sr, who called himself a wartime hero, with his slew of fake medals like bottle caps; and the flamboyant First Lady, the Nuestra Señora de Metro Manila, with her diamonds shaped like her fake tears.

After the war, Guillerma bore Alberto three children. Alberto Junior, or Jun, took up commerce at a downtown university that had an enrolment of almost 50,000 ('Asia's biggest university' its ads claimed), and such expansion could only lead to diminution in the quality of education so that, gradually, this university became a diploma mill. But they could not help sending him there— the tuition was still within their means. The result of her son's commerce degree was his employment in a drab government agency, where he sorted out papers stamped with 'Official' and sent them out from one office to another. Her second child, Victoria, took up education, setting foot in the tracks of teaching, following them in this 'noble profession'. But something happened during the years of Marcos Sr and military rule: the teachers' salaries shrank in inverse proportion to the rate of inflation (but the Gross National Product is 'rising', said the corpulent minister of public information, and in the next breath would perorate on the government's campaign 'against smut', which he pronounced as 'smooth'). The ministry of education, which used to have the biggest slice in the budget, had been elbowed out by the ministry of national defence and, yes, the ministry of public information. Victoria married a nondescript man whom Guillerma did not trust the first time she saw him—his body already shaped like the letter *C*, how could he carry the heavy burdens of the world?

But she bore him five children, who not only had to be fed and bathed but clothed, too, and sent to school. With her paltry pay as a schoolteacher and her husband's rare winnings in the small-town lottery, Victoria could not educate her children beyond high school. So, Victoria swallowed both pride and saliva, took a job as a governess for the family of a prince in the Kingdom of Saudi Arabia and taught the Arabian children their English and their table manners. She wrote every week, her long letters read to Guillerma by Jun, in whose words the old woman could feel the blistering heat of the desert, the daughter telling them that her nose had stopped bleeding when the temperature would soar beyond 100° Fahrenheit; that her employer, the prince, a true son of Allah, bless him, never touched her; that the princess herself, upon seeing that her children could parse the English language better than she could, and knew which knife to use for which dish, would occasionally give Victoria a bonus of 100 dinars. And Guillerma's third child, her dearest Brando, who was actually one of twins, but Marlon, who had been older by five minutes, died at the age of two from broncho-enteritis. Brando grew up a loner, picking fights here and there, stoically biting his lower lip when his father would punish him with a belt on his buttocks. She loved her son, but she never really understood him: she felt they were strangers to each other. Her words, his father's threats, everything fell on deaf ears. Brando ran away from home the summer after he had graduated from high school, and for many years, the family never heard from him, until one day, she received a letter in a thin, blue envelope. Her heart skipped a beat when she saw her son's familiar handwriting. She tore open the flap and her son's words tumbled before her:

—I'm working on a ship now docked in Norway, Mama. The climate's frigid, but the North Sea is here. There's an oil boom. Give my love to Papa, too, and to Kuya Jun and Ate Victoria. Being far gives one a sense of perspective: the farther I am, the closer I feel I have become to all of you . . .

The years slipped past like water between the fingers. Alberto and Guillerma retired from teaching. His family's fortunes had been whittled down by the years and he inherited nothing, save for an old, rice mill which he sold with great reluctance and pain ('I still remember the warm hum of the machines, Ima; I still see the rice grains turning from gold to white') so they could have something to tide them over in their retirement, since she knew that most of the lump sum of their retirement pay would just go to paying off the debts that had piled up through the years.

They had begun counting the grains of their days, moving from Albay to Jun's small house in a subdivision in Marikina, with his kind wife, Tina, and son, Billy. They had wanted to stay in the province, safe in the womb of the old hometown, but her children had insisted that they stay with Jun: 'If something happens to you, the doctors and hospitals in the city are always near. In the province—'

Then one night, she dreamt that all of her teeth had fallen out, one by one, leaving no blood and no pain, nothing . . . her teeth began floating in the void, like lost stars in the dark sky. A cold, tight grip on her arm tore her away from her dream. She snapped the button of the bedside lamp and light drenched her Alberto: his face crumpled in pain, fist gripping his chest. They rushed him to the hospital, but he was already dead before they could open the door of the ambulance in front of the hospital's lobby.

She sat tight inside the slow train bound for Albay, the wheels clicking rhythmically, bringing home the remains of her Alberto, back to the land he loved. Sounds rose pell-mell about them— men selling bottles of water where before, only young boys used to do this; vendors of peanuts, soft drinks, boiled eggs, fruit juices, pig's skin fried to a crisp. The forests of Quezon were slowly receding; no longer could you see a swarm of fireflies like tiny lanterns ablaze in the night. The wooden houses strung about the railroad tracks looked older and frailer than they used to be, and when the train lurched past Camarines Sur, there rose before her the volcano with the most perfect cone, Mayon, now draped in a grey casket of clouds.

And then darkness.

The whole town turned out for the burial of Alberto. His former students, some of whom were now teachers themselves, attended the five-night wake. They not only spoke of his stern discipline in the classroom, but also of his love for learning and of the life of the mind. The three daughters of Estrella, wanting to shield her from his death, did not tell her that Alberto had already died. Estrella had also begun to sink: she was almost deaf, and had become incontinent. But on the second night of the wake, the three daughters of Estrella were stunned to see their mother slowly making her way up the stone stairs of Guillerma's house. They ran to her and asked her who had told her that her friend had passed away, but she just brushed them aside. She walked straight into the living room and stopped before Alberto's coffin. Her head was bowed low. The funeral bulbs glowed around her white hair, like a halo. Guillerma walked over to her old friend and gripped her hand.

Before Estrella spoke, in a voice now no more than a whisper, Guillerma already knew what her friend would say: 'I felt Alberto's presence, Ima.' A sudden coldness clutched Guillerma. She embraced Estrella tightly as the old woman continued to speak: 'Everybody's leaving . . .'

At first, it was a persistent greyness, which Guillerma thought was just a residue of grief. But slowly, she began to see the world as through a misted windowpane. She would wipe the mist away, but instead of disappearing, it became thicker, heavier, until one day, Jun brought her to the hospital and the doctor said, 'It's all over.'

Jun later told her that he did not know how to react: Was the diagnosis over? Or was the glaucoma all over?

But she knew that the glaucoma was, indeed, all over, covering the windows of her eyes layer by layer, until one fine morning, although she could feel the sunlight making warm pools on her skin, the fine hair on her nape began to stand on end, icy sweat breaking out of her: everything had collapsed into darkness.

Being blind was like learning a new language. Again, she had to learn the alphabet of the house: a step here, and she was in the living room; a few steps there, and she was in the cool depths of the bathroom; if she took several more steps, she would be out in the backyard, beneath the mango trees.

She refused Jun's offer of a walking stick.

'That would just make me feel really old and helpless—or it would make me feel imperial and rich! Besides,' she added, 'I can use my nose.' Her sense of scent grew sharper by the day, so much so that she could smell her frisky grandson, Billy, bounding into the room, sunshine and sweat on his hair, or smell Mrs Valenzuela's chicken *adobo* whose aroma of soy sauce and vinegar would be floating from her house, or smell the smoke from the animal innards being barbecued in the food stalls of Cubao's side streets . . .

When it was time for Billy to go to school, she volunteered to bring him there every morning and pick him up in the afternoon. Jun and his wife said 'no' almost simultaneously, but they knew they could offer no other suggestion. He had a 9–5 job in Manila; she was a nurse at the V. Luna Medical Centre, with her irregular hours. She told them, holding her young grandson's palm in hers, that they would be all right.

* * *

Wanda called her lola, and every afternoon, after school, she would go to the garden and talk to the old woman. She would invite Lola inside, but the old woman preferred to stay in the garden for she loved sitting in that wooden chair, rocking it back and forth, back and forth.

Wanda offered her coffee and cookies, sometimes, a piece of the blueberry cheesecake that she would bring home from the university cafeteria, whose cakes and pastries were the only things you could eat without breaking out into a rash the next day. She would put the cake on a white saucer and offer it to Lola, who would nibble away, bit by bit, then sip her warm coffee, slowly, while unravelling her stories, unwrapping them, like gifts.

One day, Wanda told the old woman that she wanted to go abroad. 'I want to leave this country.'

'Why?' she asked.

'I can't stand it. All this mindless violence. The greed and the corruption. This country is Asia's basket case.'

'And so, do you want to *abandon* it?'

Wanda suddenly stopped, jolted by this woman. She then looked at her intensely—this old woman who was more of an apparition, a ghost, than reality. But Lola would be calm, even self-possessed. 'Lola, you don't understand. There are more opportunities abroad.'

'That's what they all say. My Victoria tells me stories of Filipina housemaids being raped by their Arabian masters, then thrown out of the windows of palaces.'

'It doesn't happen all the time.'

'In Japan, the word "Filipina" is synonymous with "prostitute".'

'The Japs have always been weird. Look at the English words they print on their T-shirts.'

'In Hong Kong, they have a doll dressed up in the uniform of a domestic helper. Of course, they call the D.H. Filipina.'

'The Hong Kong Chinese have always been arrogant. They must have forgotten that their mothers used to be *amahs*, housemaids, too, in Manila before the Second World War.'

'Brando tells me how his White co-workers, who like him also work with their hands, snigger at his accent. Then, they'd ask him if he too has holes in his palms, like those Filipinos who hang themselves on the cross every Good Friday.'

'Well, Lola, all of us are racists in one form or another. Deep in our hearts, we adore the Whites and despise the Blacks, the Indians, the Chinese—'

The old woman kept quiet, resumed sipping her coffee and nibbling her food, slowly, silently. Wanda would be glad, for she hated the feeling of being compared to a rat looking for a way out, abandoning a sinking ship.

Sometimes, in another mood, Wanda would tell the old woman stories about school, about her professor in Philippine history whose questions in their exams could easily freak you out.

Question: What was the height of our national hero, the novelist Dr Jose Rizal?

Answer: Five feet, four inches.

Question: What was the name of Dr Rizal's dog during his exile in Dapitan?

Answer: Usman.

And Lola would cackle—no, she would not laugh, she would cackle—that sound of pure joy rising from her lips and floating in the garden, before evaporating like perfume. She would shake her head vigorously, then ask, 'Are you sure you're not making this up, Wanda?' and then it would be Wanda's turn to laugh, swearing on the bones of her beloved cat, Beckett, that she was telling the truth.

She also told Lola about Stephen, her classmate, who was not really that gorgeous (hair beginning to recede in the middle—and he's only eighteen!), but who was bright, witty and sad.

'That looks like an interesting young man, Wanda. Reminds me of my Alberto.' Silence. 'I do miss my Alberto.'

'I'm sure you do, Lola. And I'm sure Lolo Alberto would like Stephen, who writes plays, which he also directs and acts.'

'Sounds like Charlie Chaplin, Wanda. We used to watch his films in film appreciation workshop in school.'

'Certainly does, Lola. But like me, he also wants to leave his house after college, go to New York and study film at New York

University, where Milos Forman teaches, then, perhaps, establish himself there.'

'Just like you, yes,' and Lola would cluck her tongue.

'Please don't feel bad, Lola, about our plans to leave the country. You know how terrible our movie industry is. Mother Tiger has completely gone over the edge. She now insists on seeing walking zombies and flying coffins in every movie she produces. And you know what, Lola? She called up Zigzag Bustamante, Stephen's brilliant film teacher and one of the country's few sane directors, she called him up at 2 a.m. It seems that she keeps a box of index cards with a list of titles arranged in alphabetical order for every movie she makes. So, she called up Zigzag at 2 a.m. and asked him to attend her press conference at her sprawling villa in Corinthian Gardens (cost: 200 million pesos). As Zigzag told Stephen, who later passed on the news to me, he was still sleepy when he arrived at the villa. It seemed like he had just come home after drinking with some friends at the Penguin Café in Manila. The press-conference room was barricaded with tables, on top of which sat many images of the Holy Infant Jesus, in brocade and gold, with sceptres and crowns studded with real diamonds, Lola. Wearing a brown kaftan that made her look like a moth, Mother Tiger grandly announced that she had reached the letter R, so her latest movie would be called *Rosebuds are Red, and So are You*. Zigzag, whose films had won acclaim from Tokyo to Berlin, just freaked out and stormed out of the villa.'

'Well, if your Stephen goes, there goes the fight. You'll just let the barbarians stay—and get richer.'

One day, Wanda told the old woman something she had not even told Stephen, who was already her boyfriend by then: her parents had decided to split up.

'Mom can't stand Dad. She says he's just a piece of junk, smelly and rotten like the junk his firm collects from around the city—paper, cartons, plastic sheets, empty bottles—

for recycling. Dad said it's a decent job and it's only one of several firms he runs, and he has built this house on his own, with not a single centavo from Mom's parents. Mom said she should have listened to her mom when she told her to dump my father . . .'

'When are they separating?' Lola asked, fixing her unseeing eyes on Wanda.

'Next month. Mom's moving to my grandparents' house in New Manila with my brother, Bombi. I get to stay with Papa. Then, Bombi and I will swap places after a month.'

'Did they talk to you about it?'

'Oh yes, they did. It was all so proper and formal that it looked like a business meeting. On one side of the long *narra* hardwood table in our library sat Dad; on the other, claiming her territory, was Mom. Bombi and I sat across from each other, fidgeting in our seats. They've divided their property—down to their collection of books and CDs—down to the last item. It was all so civilized, really.'

Lola drew a deep sigh. 'Things happen, Wanda.'

'Dad told me he can't stand Mom's snobbery, her airs of aristocracy. Mom said, "Imagine, I run my family's real-estate corporation, and during cocktail parties, everybody does stocks, jewellery, real estate and my husband *does* junk?"' Wanda tried to sound light-hearted about it, even droll and dismissive, but her voice was beginning to break. Lola raised her hand in the air, as if trying to grasp something floating there. Then, she held the hands of Wanda, who blinked once, twice. The lines on Lola's forehead were deep, the flesh sagging around her chin and arms. Her eyes were as white as bone.

'Wanda,' she said, her hand touching the young woman's cheeks, 'accept everything.' She broke the word *accept* in two, breaking it like warm bread, and offering it to Wanda. 'It's only the beginning.'

The young girl wanted to call out for Stephen, for Bombi, for her mom and dad, because something hot and grainy had begun to brush against her throat, rising in the fields of her face, blooming like clear, warm petals in her eyes.

What to do, what to do next?

Oh, Wanda survived her teenage years in two different houses, living two different lives: her father's house with its familiar tapestry of *The Last Supper* hanging on the wall of the dining room, her mother's house with its copies of *Cosmo* and *Vogue* magazines scattered casually about the mahogany coffee table. She suspected that both her parents must have had lovers, but they conducted their affairs so discreetly that the children pretended not to mind. Bombi is now taking up management engineering in the exclusive Jesuit university, robust and down-to-earth like their father. Stephen and Wanda are now living together in a small apartment in UP Village. At first, her dad was furious when Wanda told him that they had decided to live-in.

He asked, 'Why not get married?' but Wanda did not answer him. She just fixed her stare on him. Her mother, as usual, couldn't care less, especially after she met Stephen, who has gone almost bald in the middle, but he has not succumbed to Mother Tiger's juicy offer (six figures) for him to direct *Ramborat*, the Filipino version of *Rambo*.

One day, Lola simply stopped coming. The maid told Wanda that the old woman's oldest son, Jun, had dropped by to thank them, and to break the news that Lola had died in her sleep. It was so much like her: she just ebbed away silently, peacefully. Wanda attended the wake for two nights, attending for the sake of Victoria and Brando, who had managed to send money home for what Jun called 'a decent funeral'.

In the memorial park where everything was green with Bermuda grass and pine trees, after the priest had intoned the last words (*dust, ashes*), Wanda threw a brilliant pink orchid from their garden down into the pit where Lola's brown coffin was being lowered.

She turned around and walked away. In the immense eye of noon, she seemed to see Lola—singing *My bonnie lies over the ocean*; meeting Alberto for the first time in teaching methods class; giving birth to her three children; telling her young, bewildered students to accept, and to survive—she seemed to see Lola now, crossing continents, saying farewell to Victoria in the blazing heat of the desert, touching Brandon's brow in the coldness of the ship in the Arctic Circle, and then finally meeting her bonnie beyond the sea.

LOLA'S VROOM-VROOM

My *lola*, my grandmother, brought me to her hometown in Albay every summer, when I was still a kid. We would take the slow, overnight train. The train swayed from side to side. I would look outside and see colourful buntings hanging on strings for the fiesta. Or see houses warm with light from kerosene lamps. Or see children playing tag or hopscotch in the alleys. My lola just slept, but I would sometimes rest my head against her fat arms. The sound of the train was like the beating of her heart.

My lola walked with me to church every dawn of December 24th. In the chilly air, we would attend the *Misa de Gallo,* the midnight Mass before the stroke of midnight signalled the coming of Christmas. I would cling to her hand as we walked in the dark. I was never afraid of the dark as long as she was with me. Her hand was warm.

My lola taught us to cook dried taro leaves in coconut milk. Dried fish and small shrimps would be mixed in that lake of coconut milk. Sliced onions, crushed garlic, and small cubes of ginger would already be there, simmering in the vat of coconut milk. And then, the dried taro leaves and stems would follow. Her face would almost vanish in the steam rising from the coconut milk. And the smell of the food would perfume the whole house.

These were what I saw and smelt and heard and tasted in my mind, when I looked outside the bus bringing me home to my lola. Earlier, I had received a text message. 'Please go home,' it said, 'something happened to Lola.'

I got off in front of the subdivision. I walked to our house. When I reached our house, it was quiet.

My lola had been sick during the past month. She was ninety years old. One morning, we found her sprawled on the floor. Black marks like maps had formed on her skin.

We lifted her up, back on to her bed.

'What happened, Lola?' I asked.

'I was just trying to stand up . . . when I fell,' she said in a weakened voice.

We brought her to the hospital. The doctor said her brittle bones had broken. He said she must have already fallen several times before we found her. She was trying to get back to her bed.

'It's like the old branches of a tree finally breaking,' the doctor said.

She refused a wheelchair. She just lay in bed at home and took the medicines the doctor had prescribed for her. 'It is painful. My knees and my joints,' she once told me, holding my hand tightly. 'Everything is painful. How I wish . . . your Lolo were here.'

I would feed her and ask her to sip water from a glass. Then, I would run my fingers over her forehead. She used to do this to me when I was young, when I was waiting for my parents to come home from work. Her presence was something that always gave me comfort. But her arms that used to be fat now had loose skin. She was already thin.

* * *

After I opened the gate of our house, I wanted to rush into her room. But, as I was entering the house, I almost bumped into Luigi. He was my two-year-old nephew. In the past few weeks, we had been teaching him how to walk.

And now, he could not only walk, he was even running out to meet me, startling the morning around him. I lifted him and kissed him on the cheek.

'Where is Lola?' I asked him.

'Wowa?' he said.

Then he turned his head in the direction of grandmother's room. I put Luigi down and held his hand. We walked into the living room. It was then that I saw Auntie Millet.

'Your Lola has died,' she said. As simple as that. Red veins seemed to form in her eyes. Tears gleamed in her face.

A lump of stone grew in my throat. Something sharp stung my eyes. I sat beside Lola's bed. I touched her forehead. I ran my fingers over her hair. Her hair had turned completely white, like abaca fibres.

During the funeral wake, our family and friends came. From near and far, they gathered to pay their respects to Lola. She was in a white coffin surrounded by wreaths of orchids and lighted bulbs.

When Luigi came, he immediately ran to me and asked, 'Vrroom, vroom?' indicating the sound of a car. His eyes were looking at the casket surrounded by the brilliant lights. 'Wowa?' he asked.

'Yes,' I answered. 'Vroom. Vroom. Lola is about to go on ahead of us.'

'Leaving . . . us?' he asked, his eyes narrowing.

'Yes, but we will see her again,' I assured him. 'One day we will.'

Then, I embraced Luigi and lifted him. I brought him to his Lola, so he could look at her face in the coffin and say his final goodbye.

THE GIRL WHO LOVED
THE BEATLES

Myrna was my mother's student in grade VI, a girl who sat quietly in class, read her textbooks and passed. She went to the local public school, and for college, her parents sent her to Manila, since she was the eldest. After her graduation, she was expected to work and, in turn help her siblings get their college degrees. Her father, *Mang* Johnny, was a robust soldier who served as the sacristan to the military chaplain every Sunday, for the 8 a.m. and 5 p.m. Masses. Thus, he went to Mass at least twice every Sunday, and in my young mind, I realized that that gave him enough indulgences to ensure for him a room in heaven.

But now, Myrna was back from Manila after only one semester of taking up business administration in a downtown university. She was in her room, surrounded by children like me, while her mother and brother held her down. The wizened old woman who was standing at the foot of the bed was moving her lips, uttering something in pidgin Latin. In front of her was a burning white candle atop a brass holder stolen from the chapel. Over the flame, the old woman held a white plate, with its face down.

Then Myrna's voice floated in the room as she sang 'Hey Jude'. Her voice was clear and bright; the words of the song seemed to touch the very walls of her room. Her eyes were focused on the ceiling, on an image only she could see.

Her mother was close to tears, running her fingers through her daughter's hair, wiping the sweat off her forehead with a white handkerchief. Through it all, her younger brother, all of sixteen, stood stoic.

'It's over,' the old woman said. At that, we all rushed to Myrna, gathering around her in a tight circle. Myrna seemed to have been drained of all strength, for she just uttered a cry, then wilted and fell into a deep sleep. The old woman, who smelt of my grandmother's White Flower medicine, slowly turned the plate, face up. And on the plate, a figure had been drawn: a conical hat, pointed nose, and chin with a long beard. It was sharply drawn, charcoal black against the white plate.

We all gasped. *Duende*, we said, the murmur spreading around us. Gravely the old woman said, 'A dwarf in your backyard must have taken a fancy to Myrna. He lives in that tall mound of earth at the foot of the banana tree.'

'What must we do?' the mother asked. 'My daughter hasn't eaten anything in two days. She vomits the food and speaks in a language we can't understand.'

'There's a mischievous dwarf inside her,' intoned the old woman. 'You can only appease him by burying three brown, native chicken's egg beside the dwarf's house.'

Myrna's mother followed the old woman's advice, but the next morning, Myrna's name was again on everybody's lips. It was past midnight, and their neighbour, Aling Naty, had just finished pressing their clothes for the week. She wanted to take in some fresh air, so she walked over to the window. And she could not believe what she saw when she looked out of the window.

'JesusMaryJoseph!' she shouted, and her husband, Mang Teddy, was soon by her side. Mang Teddy once called me a sissy to my face (I don't know why; I was so butch) when nobody was around. I felt my ears turning into flames. But how do you get back at a man twice your height and thrice your age? He played the trumpet for the military band. That was why he had such big balls, said one wag. In my mind, I wished those balls would grow bigger than watermelons so they could be easy targets for my trusted slingshot.

But that night, Myrna stood in the middle of the street, beside a massive acacia tree. She was stark naked in the moonlight. I was not sure how Mang Teddy's balls responded to that. But he had difficulty following his wife, who had run down the stairs to drape a colourful blanket of red-and-orange stripes around the young woman's body. She brought her home and although Aling Naty tried to make Myrna speak, no words came from the young woman's lips.

Matilda lived near Myrna's house, and we called her Matilda, the *Maldita*, or the wicked one. We also called her the 'motor mouth' because words zipped from her mouth at a fast clip. She said that Myrna only did all of these strange things because she wanted to grab people's attention.

Connie, another neighbour, who also studied in Manila, thought that Myrna might have a drug problem. 'That's why I avoid parties,' she sniffed. 'A boy might put something in your drink; then he'll play with you all night long. After you've been damaged, nobody will want you any more,' she added daintily, her fingers fluttering on her neck.

'Or perhaps, she's just depressed because the Beatles have disbanded?' suggested another classmate.

'Whatever—' said Matilda with finality, and then tossed her head, her black hair full of split ends.

Through it all, Mang Johnny continued working from Monday to Friday, then served the Lord every Sunday. He did bring his daughter to Doctor Dacanay at the military airbase, who found nothing wrong with her—neither pregnant nor mad. He just prescribed rest and a lot of sleep.

'Perhaps she has not yet adjusted to Manila's fast pace at university?' Doctor Dacanay pressed on.

Her father sent her home to Albay in the Bicol Region, to have a break and take in fresher air. The sight of the blue sea, he thought, and the salt in the wind would do her good. A year later, she returned to Manila and finished her course. Two years after graduation, she even got a scholarship for a master's in business administration at the highly regarded Asian Institute of Management. She now worked as the chief accountant for a multinational company in the central business district of Makati, the oasis where everybody wanted to be.

Once, after more than ten years of absence, she went home for a visit. She went home briefly to bury her father, who had died peacefully in his sleep. I saw her at the funeral wake held at the chapel of the military airbase. She was standing in front of his white casket. Two young soldiers stood guard on both ends of the coffin, giving military honours to her late father. The tricolour of the Philippine flag was draped around his coffin.

In her blue designer suit, the pearls cooling her neck, her long hair swept in a stylish bun, I tried to look for her: the girl who sang 'Hey Jude' in a voice cut with shadows, the girl who once walked naked in a night washed with moonlight.

But the woman before me was no longer young and lonely. Finally, the world was now in the palm of her hand.

THE YOUNG EMMANUEL

Emmanuel was a young man from the windblown island of K, in the eastern part of Luzon, a small island seemingly adrift in the Pacific Ocean, as if it were in a dream. After graduating valedictorian from the provincial high school, where he edited the student organ called *The Mighty Pen,* he applied for a journalism scholarship at the Royal and Pontifical University of Santo Tomas. He was accepted.

Now, the Dominicans had not yet fully recovered from the routing of the Spanish clergy at the turn of the century. Still, they walked about the sprawling grounds of the university as if they bustled about the old hacienda: everything, everything as far as the eyes could see, would be theirs. Still, they hewed closely to the rigors of the old Vatican, closely monitoring the books that their students were reading, making sure that the students did not read anything that had been included in the *Index of Forbidden Books.* They grudgingly admitted women into the university because of dipping finances.

They accepted the female students who, of course, were separated from the men. Thus, you had one university with two wings, for him and for her, and a strict and bearded old South Asian who had been tasked with ensuring that no one talked to the women.

Why a South Asian?

Perhaps in the weird psychology of the dominant, er, Dominican Order, the men and women now strolling the university grounds were still just boys and girls who had grown up. In their minds they still feared the 'Bombay'—tall, dark-skinned, and hairy; a beard and moustache around the lips; eyes sunk in silence; a turban wound around the head. The old Bombay of childhood memory, the ambulant businessman who, the housemaids had said, liked to kidnap children, put them inside sacks, and later sell them.

* * *

Into the vortex of that world the young Emmanuel plunged, finding the city as if it were another world. But soon he grew tired of school—of teachers who constantly asked him to parrot their answers, who completely and uncouthly ignored his questions in class, who gossiped scandalously about their neighbours one moment and stood still as saints in Mass.

Moreover, the scholarship only paid for tuition, miscellaneous fees and books, and he still had to ask for an allowance from his mother in K. His father had died when Emmanuel was only five years old, swept upriver by a tropical cyclone on his way home, and his mother, a public-school teacher, brought him up on her own. Even if she had only one child to raise, still she felt that every payday, her pockets had holes through which her salary fell. She could only save enough money for the young Emmanuel by denying herself the basic things: she went to work in her old shoes, the patent leather beginning to crack; she ate the vegetables which she grew in her backyard, sometimes mixing them with *hibe*, the small dried shrimps which she bought cheaply in small plastic bags in the public market; she had no television set and only listened to the radio for the announcement of another tropical cyclone blowing in from the Pacific Ocean, learning this lesson keenly after her husband's death.

The young Emmanuel knew this, and so one day he turned up at the office of the *Evening Express*, then the country's top-circulation broadsheet, and asked to see the editor-in-chief.

* * *

Mr Nilo Perez was small, brown and rotund. When he looked up from the pile of manuscripts on his desk, he reminded Emmanuel of a rat.

In between his words, he constantly sniffed. Emmanuel showed him an essay he had written in school, which he had scribbled off ten minutes before class began and which had gotten him a flat A from his teacher, to his great elation and dismay. Flanked by the photos of the dictator and his wife, the editor-in-chief read the essay, his fingers flying over the page, and then he looked at the young Emmanuel with rapturous eyes: 'I like it! You know how to write. You began with a quotation. And you ended with one. It's a perfect circle.'

The young Emmanuel fidgeted in his seat (*God, the world is full of morons*), and smiled his PR smile, the one he had practised every day before the mirror: a wide smile that fully showed his white teeth, a smile without meaning.

So, the young Emmanuel was hired and the next day, he began writing 'think pieces' for the *Express*. 'What makes Filipino culture tick?' was balanced the next day with a witty essay on 'The heritage of Op-Ed columnists with big egos'.

After that, letters began pouring into the *Express* in praise of this wunderkind. The young Emmanuel was promoted to editorial writer and assistant editor (much to the chagrin and envy of the senior editors). Thus, he was able to buy long-sleeved shirts, no longer from Quiapo's bazaars but in cool Escolta's shops, and send money every month to his mother.

* * *

One day, the dictator's information minister, Gorgonio Balbacua, died. Minister Balbacua had an appetite for sex matched only by his incredible diction. On nationwide telly he was quoted, 'We should wage a nationwide campaign against smut and all forms of pornography.' He pronounced smut as 'smooth'. His ghost writers, a group of highly paid brats from Manila's most exclusive universities, had a grand time trawling polysyllables for the boss. Asterisks became 'Asterix', labyrinthine was lost and by the time he had reached 'anthropomorphism' (delivered before a group of society matrons who raised tiger orchids as a hobby and whose avowed aim was to 'Exterminate All Aphids'), the minister's tongue was gone.

But his ghost writers were children of the social register themselves, and thus, could not be fired.

So, he just vented all his frustrations on his sex life. His latest gamine was Ylang-Ylang, the lead star of that monstrous hit called *Nympha*. Ylang-Ylang had long, black hair that cascaded down her body like a caress, and she ruled over the dark movie houses of Manila with her voice. Low and throaty, it was a voice perfect for purring, for teasing and for titillating . . .

* * *

Furious was how the dictator acted when he heard about how the information minister had died. The minister was in Tagaytay City, inside the villa he owned, which had an unforgettable view of Taal Volcano, a volcano within a lake within a volcano within a lake, another of those conundrums in this country of so much fantasy. 'Imagine,' the dictator fumed, 'dying while in the middle of sex?'

'At least he died happy,' the wags said, buying their tabloids and horse-race guides and listening to the double entendres from the mad commentators on the AM radio band.

Thus, the vacancy. The shortlisted candidates included Mr Juan Gabuna, who was the editor-in-chief of *Asia Magazine*, the continent's finest; Professor Justiniani Culiculi, who taught at the University of the Philippines and whose posh accent never failed to remind you that, indeed, he had read the classics at Oxford University; and the young Emmanuel, who was the dark horse.

Mr Gabuna politely turned down the offer, saying he had just signed another five-year contract with *Asia Magazine*. Pundits claimed that Mr Gabuna, who used to write prize-winning fiction in his youth, would rather edit Asia's most elegant magazine than write fiction for the dictator.

Professor Culiculi also said 'No, thank you' after the palace ruled that if he were chosen for the post, he could not bring his pet poodle, Fifi, into the office.

Thus, the mantle, as the speakers would say during graduation ceremonies, fell on the young Emmanuel's shoulders.

* * *

He took to it gladly, like a diver plunging into cool, clear depths. He brought dynamism into the office. At least, the government's press releases now spell 'occasion' correctly, the letterhead doesn't have a leaking pen for a logo and the secretaries no longer pad around the place in their cheap flip-flops from the night market of Baclaran.

When the dictator finally declared martial law, to fully tighten the noose around the neck of his beloved country, it was the young Emmanuel's task to become an anti-perspirant and anti-deodorant rolled into one.

'Ahem,' he said in solemn tones over a nationwide radio and television hook-up, which we watched on the night of 23 September 1972. But he was a letdown. He just repeated the dictator's words from the previous day, his eyes like the eyes of a statue. 'The president had declared martial law to save the republic from the Communists and to form a new society.' That would be the mantra of the military dictatorship for many days and nights, for the dictatorship seemed to last forever.

Just then, Emmanuel produced a list. 'Here are the names of the undesirable elements in our society. To protect the interests of the State, they have been placed in rehabilitation centres.' And he proceeded to read out the names of 7,000 people, deep into the night and early the next morning, his voice a monotone. Every so often he would bend down and pull up his socks (a tic, someone said, because the Young Emmanuel used to go to school with rubber bands wound around the sagging bands of his socks). And sometimes, one could see a dagger of fear in those big, intelligent eyes—or could it just be sleepiness?—as his voice droned on and on in the archipelago.

The moment my father fell asleep on the sofa at midnight, I turned off the television set. Young Emmanuel disappeared into the void of the idiot box, and vanished to the point of a small white dot, as my weary countrymen turned off their television sets one by one and braced themselves for another longer night.

THE RUINED HOTEL

The wind was already cold as a knife against the skin when we arrived at the mountain city of Baguio, in northern Philippines. Mang Senyong, the school-bus driver said as we were alighting from the bus, 'Don't forget to ask the Spirit Warriors for the winning lotto numbers.' He gave his reminder to us with his trademark smirk, and then he grinned widely, his front teeth yellowed with nicotine.

'Of course,' answered Lito, one of the members of the academic staff who had attended the newsletter-writing session up here in Baguio. 'Then we can all share the prize of P250 million for the mega lotto!' The rest of the people in the bus—mostly academic staff and I, the visiting journalist—snickered. Of course, I thought a lotto windfall would be welcome. Since times had been bad—what with the peso pegged at 60 to a US dollar, rice selling at 100 pesos a kilo, and every other Filipino wanting to work overseas as a caregiver—a deep depression had begun to grip the country.

I checked the time in my slim, square watch. 10 p.m. The air chilled me the moment I got off the air-conditioned school bus. Why, I thought, it's even colder out here in the open air than inside that bus! It was December and we were in Baguio City for a workshop on newsletter publishing. Etta, the dean of the university—a tall, talkative woman who was my classmate at Saint Theresa's College—had asked me to train her staff.

I took a break from copyediting articles by twenty-something upstarts who thought that their prose was witty ('Bohol-licious food on the island of Bohol') or society columns on where they could find the fluffiest feather boa for the next party. Good Lord, where have all the writers gone?

It was also a visit I had been hesitant to make. I had just broken up with Jey (short for Jeyaretnam), my Indian boyfriend, a year ago. I met him in one of those ASEAN conferences where journalists update each other on bilateral relations and the ASEAN-Plus Protocols. I was standing near the coffee stand when this tall and good-looking gentleman said, 'Excuse me,' and got the milk for his cup of tea.

Being Filipina, I smiled at him and he smiled back and that was how we began to talk. He had studied at University College in London, in a programme that mixed diplomacy with journalism and political science. He won me over with his elegant accent and deep baritone, as well as his keen mimicry of the favourite words spoken by the Filipinos he had met in the United Kingdom. Our new heroes, the *Bagong Bayani*, our overseas Filipino workers—the entertainers, housemaids and carpenters—taught their foreigner friends a gaggle of words ranging from *How are you?* to the unprintable ones. It didn't hurt that Jey also looked like a Bollywood movie star, and he was the most courteous man I had ever met.

He always punctuated his words with 'I'm sorry', his eyes deep and glistening, his moustache and beard black as night. He was always asking me what I wanted, whether we were in a fine-dining restaurant or at the bustling mall or lining up in the cinema houses. Unlike Filipino men, who were spoilt rotten by their mothers, Jey had worked his way to graduate school and knew all the household chores, from cooking the best curry to pressing the clothes without any creases.

In short, he would have been the perfect husband—or the perfect butler. I loved him with a passion, even if my friends sometimes teased me for being 'The Curry Queen' because I suddenly fell in love with a South Asian. In December of last year, Jey visited Manila on a brief holiday. We went to Baguio City because he found the noxious air of Manila bad for his asthma. We avoided Session Road since it was also crowded with people and choked with diesel fumes. We stayed in a cosy and quiet hotel in the suburbs. He laughed mightily, his voice rolling inside the small store in the public market, when I pulled down the wooden barrel and the wooden figure's dick sprang to life for all the world to see. He looked away from the young boys from the indigenous tribes, wearing loincloths and dancing below the cliff, then catching the rain of coins thrown by the tourists in Mines' View Park.

Big glass jars of purple yam and strawberry jam filled our bags as we left the convent of the Good Shepherd nuns. Our fingers entwined, we strolled in Burnham Park and on the wide pedestrian walks, marvelling at the sunflowers which were following the path of the sun. And in the hotel room, after the deep conversation and the hugs and the warm words whispered into each other's ears, we made love, the gentle and urgent love-making that left me in tears at first. Will this love last? I asked myself. And when I looked outside, in the deep night of December, the windows were beginning to be covered with fog.

* * *

But this December, a year later, I was again in Baguio City because Etta was the kind of friend who would wake up from her sleep and listen to your sob story at 4 a.m. Thus, I could not turn down her request for me to train their academic staff. At the end of our dinner a fortnight ago, while sipping her favourite cappuccino, she even told me, 'Well, it's been a year since you and your Indian gentleman went to Baguio City. I think it's time you return and bury the bones of that beast!'

I laughed my usual laughter—a cackle, really, like a hen about to lay a big, fat egg—although a black veil suddenly fell over my face. And then I knew that the pain—or residues of it—still remained.

* * *

But today, I was going down the bus to watch the Spirit Warriors at the Baguio Terraces Hotel. The staff wanted to see the Spirit Warriors appease the spirits that allegedly still roamed the premises of the hotel. Or what used to be the hotel. For now, in front of me, was just a wall of galvanized-iron sheets painted green, enclosing the area where the Baguio Terraces Hotel used to be. Lito knocked and a guard in a white-and-blue uniform opened the gate.

The ruins of the hotel where almost 500 people died (nobody was sure about the exact body count) had been cleared. Not a stone remained standing. And the Spirit Warriors were already there—a group of teenagers half my age together with Marlon, their mentor. Marlon, my friend, was also a writer of amazing fiction about elves and other supernatural creatures roaming the city. He walked over to us and said, 'Lisa, you cannot just watch the Spirit Warriors. We want the observers to be participants as well. You and the lady beside you should go there!' Marlon pointed to a place shrouded in darkness.

Melody, the secretary of the department of English, held my hand. With reluctance, I followed her and ten teenagers in the direction that Marlon had indicated. It was in a spot on the northern part of the street. I had been stupid enough to not bring my cardigan, and so in my plain T-shirt I shivered as I walked. When I looked up, the stars seemed to shiver as well, in the thick and cold darkness of the sky.

'Let us sit down and form a circle in this area,' Ding-Dong, our leader, said, tapping the ground with the end of his rough, wooden cane. We obeyed. 'God of Light,' he began to chant. He repeated this thrice and then stopped suddenly. 'Someone is here.'

I looked to my left, then to my right. But there was nobody around.

Ding-Dong continued speaking, but in a more formal tone. 'Good evening. We are here at the Baguio Terraces Hotel because we've been asked to help the spirits still roaming in this place.'

Silence.

Ding-Dong explained in a softer, conspiratorial voice: 'The woman asked me who I am, so I told her about us.' Then, he continued speaking to the darkness beyond. 'There was a major earthquake here ten years ago, with an intensity of 7.5. The hotel was completely destroyed—I'm sorry, but you were among those who had died.'

Silence.

The voice of Ding-Dong began to rise. He seemed agitated. I saw his grip on the cane tighten. 'She is angry with us. She says I'm lying! Quick, let's share our own pain with her to make her understand she's not alone in her suffering. We've to empathize with her. Okay, you first,' he added, pointing at the girl who sat across from me.

'Okay,' the girl said. 'Good evening.' In a Valley Girl accent, she said, 'I wanna share my pain with you, Miss. Coz, you know, one time, I went home really super late and kinda drunk so my dad and mom grounded me. They didn't allow me to drive my car for a week.' Then the tone of her voice began to rise. 'It was so painful coz, you know, I had to take public transport for one week. It was kinda hell for me!'

I looked at Barbie and wished the ground beneath her feet would just open and swallow her up.

'Is there anybody else who wants to share her pain?' Ding-Dong asked. 'Quick, guys, because she is now driving us away!'

'Well,' began the boy to the left of Barbie. He was a Filipino-American with long and layered hair, like a Korean pop singer's. He was wearing a new denim jacket in full-blooded blue. 'I failed calculus last sem and my parents, you know how strict they are, right? They didn't take me with them when they went to Europe. I had to take up calculus again during summer classes. I had to stay at home and swim in our pool at home.'

Maybe piranhas should be let loose in that pool, I thought. But I just looked at him without flinching.

Suddenly, my thighs and legs felt like they were being punctured by so many pins and needles. It was followed by a heaviness that fell on my nape and my shoulders. Later, I felt as if a boulder had been placed on my entire back. My head was beginning to swell. Then I began to see her, amorphous at first, like smoke, then turning into something solid, visible.

She is wearing a white, long-sleeved shirt. Her blue jeans are faded. She is sitting on a brown sofa with soft cushions. She is asleep. There is a sudden jolt, which makes her sofa quickly dart to the right. She wakes up with a start. People are running before her. She sees them as if in a blur. And when she looks up, the ceiling is already crashing down on her.

But she thinks it is just a dream. She has been waiting for Jeremy to come home from the convent of the Good Shepherd nuns. Jeremy likes purple yam and strawberry jam, and their stock has run short. She is waiting for Jeremy because, when he comes back, they will take a walk. They will walk in the park and on the roadside, in the cool, bracing air, and admire the sunflowers following the path of the sun.

I did speak to her. I do not know why, but I did. When I spoke to her, my voice seemed to come from a source deeper than blood and bone. I told her that she must let go. I told her that she was not dreaming. A strong earthquake ripped through the island of Luzon. The hotel crumbled. Nobody amongst the hotel guests survived the sudden crash of concrete slabs and iron bars. The earthquake happened ten years ago.

And then I told her, I do not know why, but I did; in a voice like black and bitter water, that my boyfriend, Jey, would never return as well. He had been diagnosed with leukaemia. All the blood in his body had to be drained and then a fresh infusion had to be pumped back into his system. Every six months. The cocktail of drugs that he was taking had bloated his body. The pain must have been insufferable. But he never told me about it. He just sent a text message at dawn, a year ago. I read it at dawn when I woke up to go to the toilet. My eyes were still heavy with sleep.

'I have an email for you,' the message read. I thought I was just being tugged away in a dream. I turned off my cell phone and turned it on again. I was sure the message would be gone the moment I re-activated the phone. But the words were still there; white letters like flames in the void. In the half-light cast by my bedside lamp, I fumbled for my laptop and turned it on. I read his email. The words were scissors that cut my intestines into shreds.

Leukaemia. Cannot marry you. Don't want you to take care of me. Have to go. Do not call. Do not text. Do not write to me anymore. Have a great life. Good luck.

Good luck.

Like he was a guest speaker at a graduation ceremony, and he was just wishing a thousand, fresh-faced, young people, 'Good luck. I hope all of your dreams will come true.'

End of message.

In the days that followed, I felt like the tiny, white dot on the old television screen, getting smaller and smaller until it finally vanished into the void. But I still reported for work in the office, hoping the workload would deaden me. And when my eyes would blur,

I would walk calmly to the bathroom, shut the door and silently say the words I had wanted to fling at him; Fuck you, Jey! Filipinas make the best caregivers. You didn't even give me a chance, you shithead!

But the world did not crumble. Days slipped into weeks, stretched into months, and now it had been a year. The empty room inside me had begun to shrink . . .

Suddenly, I began to shiver. My hand clutched at my chest. It was painful, as if a strong fist had gripped my heart and was squeezing it again and again. My shirt was already wet with the tears I didn't know I had begun to shed.

In the chaos, I heard Melody talking, 'Ma'am? Ma'am? Are you all right, ma'am?'

Just then, I felt a bolt of red fire streak from my heart. It zigzagged down my intestines, down to my toes, then it went up again. Its movement was swift but painful. In a flash, the red fire streaked past my head, erupting through a small hole. Its torch of light shot up into the sky.

'She has left,' Ding-Dong said just in time, 'she has moved on to the next world.'

Melody was hugging me. She was wiping my face with her handkerchief. She kept asking, 'What happened, ma'am? Are you okay, ma'am?'

I took her handkerchief and wiped my nose and chin. I looked at her. I felt so drained, as if I had just come from a faraway place. 'Nothing, Melody. I—nothing happened to me.'

Melody just nodded and tried to smile. The teenagers also asked me if I was all right.

'I'm fine,' I said. I checked the time. I looked at my slim, square watch. It was almost one in the morning.

* * *

Back at the hotel, I sat in the restaurant and ordered a cup of decaffeinated Earl Grey tea. I knew this was not the proper way to drink tea, defanged of its bergamot and its bite. But I just wanted to calm down and to have a good sleep afterwards. After finishing the cup of tea, I went up the elevator and walked back to my room on the fourth floor. I shut the windows, bolted the door and turned off the lights. When I looked outside, I saw the trees in the solid darkness. I thought somebody was waving at me, but I decided it was just the leaves awakened by a sudden breeze.

And sleep I did after a few minutes—the kind of sleep I had not had in a year, a sleep long and deep, and hardly troubled by dreams.

THE SNAKE

I once lived in a three-bedroom unit in an elegant condominium in Simei, in Singapore. My two flatmates were fellow Filipinos: Antonio was an engineer, while Roberto was a chef. I was here to write a book about Southeast Asian rivers.

On our left lived a Chinese family, the Cheongs, who sometimes had relatives visiting them. They would play mahjong until the wee hours of the morning. But the clackety-clack of the tiles did not bother me. In fact, they reminded me of my aunts who also played this game. On my right lived an Indian family, and the smell of their cooking—curries, especially *kuruma*—also wafted into my bedroom. But that didn't bother me either, for I devoured the Indian food in the restaurants near the Mass Rapid Transit train station.

In front of me lived a Malay couple, and they were very quiet indeed. When I first saw the husband, he asked me whether I was a Filipino. When I said 'yes', he said that they have Filipino carpenters in Sabah. 'But in the Philippines,' he sniffed, 'they claim to be engineers.' I just gave him my fake Filipino smile.

* * *

Mrs Cheong often talked to me. I first met her the day after I moved in. I was leaving the flat at 9 a.m. to go to the National

University of Singapore to do research when I saw her entering their flat. I gave her my genuine Filipino smile and she smiled back.

'Ah-yah, sorry-lah. We were noisy last night with mahjong.' I told her why I was not bothered, and she just smiled back.

The next week, I met her when I was going to the pool to swim. She had just finished swimming, her short hair like a grey cap over her head. 'Nice day for swimming,' she said.

I smiled back at her, 'Yes, ma'am.'

'Ah-yah. Just call me auntie-lah. You remind me of my son in Boston. Tall and thin, with glasses,' she smiled sadly.

'How many children, Auntie?'

'Only two. Alvin in Boston, Christine in Sydney. Both studying. I hope they come back.'

'I'm sure they will,' I said, thinking who wouldn't want to come back to Singapore? It had clean and tree-lined streets, and the new trains were cool and arrived on time. Everything is green here, I thought, everything is measured.

'You never know with the young ones. They think differently from me and your uncle.' Uncle I rarely saw, for he worked long hours at a bank near Clarke Quay.

One day, Auntie invited me to have lunch in their flat. She said she had cooked a lot, but their relatives could not come at the last minute, so we should eat up. Her flat had sleek, white furniture from Ikea, and we ate her soft Hainanese chicken.

We were having green tea in delicate, white cups when she told me what happened in her former flat. One of her neighbours—a tall Chinese woman whose husband also worked in a bank—turned up her nose at everyone. 'Maybe because her husband is VP in a bank and mine is merely a senior director,' she said, rolling her eyes.

'The Goh family lived in the penthouse, the most expensive in the condo. She always snubbed me,' Auntie cackled. 'But I just ignored her, too. Who cared? But one afternoon, I just heard her screaming!'

'What happened?'

'She knocked on my door. She said she had been about to use the loo when she found a snake—a thin, green snake, one foot long—in her toilet bowl. How did it reach her penthouse? Ay-yah! How would I know, lah?'

THE TWO WOMEN OF
BANTAYAN

A block away from our house beside the river stood a small house made of wood and stone. Ludy, our housemaid, told us to avoid this house. 'Aling Barang,' she said, referring to the woman living in the house, 'kidnaps children and imprisons them in her house. She always keeps her windows closed,' she added, and before our children's eyes rose the image of her windows, tightly shuttered even on the hottest days.

'It's because she would keep the children inside her house,' she continued, 'and then she would stab them in the chest, drain their blood and drink it.' A collective cry came from us, my two siblings and I. Gooseflesh crawled on our skin. 'And you know what she does to the bones of the children?'

I drew closer to our housemaid, whose nostrils flared wider at the sudden and delicious turn of her tale. 'She grinds the bones again and again until they have been reduced to grains.' Her eyes would widen for dramatic effect, and then she would end with a flourish: 'She would add this to the food she eats every day. This is her all-around additive, to improve the flavour of the food she ate every day,' she ended.

* * *

Having been sufficiently warned, we avoided that house, looking away when we passed by it, or running away the moment somebody opened the door.

But one day, I did see her. I was walking home in the late afternoon and the sun was beginning to die, when her doorway opened. Even the depths of her house seemed dark. Aling Barang stepped out quietly, with no sound at all, as if she had floated from her floor to her front yard. She looked smaller than I had imagined her to be, her long grey hair loose around her bony shoulders. Her dress had faded to a very light shade of blue, and as she approached, I stopped the impulse to run. Closer and closer she came to me, and when she was near, I saw no ferocity in her eyes. She just looked tired. She had thin hands, the skin around them beginning to blotch with age. Her bony fingers looked as if they could not swat a fly even if they tried.

But still, I remembered our housemaid's tale and I walked away as fast as I could. I was afraid that she would be hovering behind me, her snake-like hair coiling around me, her mouth exhaling breath audibly on my neck.

* * *

Near the *talipapa*, the open-air market, of the same village, lived Aling Bekang. She had left her incorrigible drunkard of a husband in town and from then on, took care of her nine children, one of whom was a young soldier.

Nine children? you might ask. The whole neighbourhood was mildly titillated when Aling Bekang began living with a man half her age—Oswaldo, or Weng-Weng for short. And the mild titillation turned to plain shock when Aling Bekang announced to everybody in the talipapa, before her stall of the greenest vegetables and the yellowest fruits, that she was pregnant.

'But, but—' Aling Pacing, who sold the longest bananas in this side of the world, which were shaped like scimitars, was about to say something.

But Aling Bekang beat her to it. 'Why, I'm only forty and I can still bear more children. You see, Weng-Weng wants to be a father now, and what he wants, he certainly gets.' The crowd at the talipapa fell into a hush. But they were surprised as the days passed because Aling Bekang's belly did not grow. To their enquiries she would always say, 'It's going to be a tiny baby.'

Aling Bekang didn't show up for months after she had made her declaration. Then, one fine day, when the sky was polished like an eggshell, the news went around that she had already given birth. The curious and the sincere went to visit her hut and found beside her bed a round, glass jar, half-filled with water.

'Hello, everyone,' she began. 'Thanks for coming to visit me. I didn't have difficulty giving birth.'

Of course, the kibitzers wanted to say, it's your tenth after all, but since they didn't want to sound impertinent, their eyes just roved around the small room. The thin walls were plastered with posters and calendars of the Christ child, robed in red, and the Blessed Virgin Mary garbed in white and blue.

When they could not contain themselves any longer, they asked: 'Where's your baby?'

She looked at them, her face filled with surprise. 'Oh, my baby is here, beside me. Can't you see my youngest baby?' she asked, pointing to the glass jar beside her. Inside it, a small, brown-black mudfish was swimming, gliding gracefully from one side of her small space to the other. The crowd thought it was a joke. Their faces cracked into wide smiles, and they slapped their thighs and laughed.

'But I'm not joking,' said Aling Bekang. 'In fact, I already have a name for her. Jezebel. And I've asked Father Agapito to baptize her two Sundays from now. Of course, you're all invited to the baptism.'

'And what did Father Agapito, er, say?' This query came from Aling Maring.

'Oh,' Aling Bekang answered, smirking, 'he said he'll think about it.'

The news about the woman who had given birth to a mudfish fire-crackered around the town, spread to the province and the region, and lofted itself into the national news.

More photographers and reporters from the tabloids came, not minding the eight-hour drive from Cebu City to Bogo City, then taking a ferry for another two hours before arriving at the white sandy beach of Bantayan. Then later, even those from the English-language broadsheets visited the house of Aling Bekang. And after that came an army of bloggers, who now called themselves 'influencers', young and brash and seemingly brainy, with their pert noses up in the air. They all crowded around her, taking photos and shooting videos of Aling Bekang cradling the glass jar. As usual, Jezebel just swam in seeming contentment inside the glass jar, taking bits and pieces of the rice bran that had been sprinkled on the surface of the water. Weng-Weng, the father, even posed for shots of himself kissing the glass jar.

'See?' he told the photographers after the photo and video shoot. 'We look alike. We even have the same lips.' Much later came the parachute journalists, the Americans with their easy banter, the British who spoke with pebbles in their mouths, and the Japanese, who never stopped taking videos.

Aling Bekang found her photographs and those of Jezebel, or rather, her glass jar, splashed on the front pages of the daily newspapers. The circulation of the tabloids that covered the news every day zoomed, and the views on the bloggers' sites rose exponentially at the startling news of Jezebel, the mudfish.

The news competed with those of the poet who talked to extra-terrestrial creatures in Laguna, the chicken that was born with three spindly legs in Pangasinan and the boy with a bloody face who talked to the Blessed Virgin Mary—but only in the King's English.

But even the extra-terrestrial creatures and the Blessed Virgin Mary did not appear regularly, unlike Jezebel, who was there for all the world to see, in living and vivid colours, images frozen in print or dynamic on video, and so the whole country revolved around the universe of this very precious jar of glass.

However, before a priest called Father Johnny Barron could baptize her as the newest member of a sect that would certainly survive the next millennium, Jezebel died. The cause of death: her glass jar accidentally tipped over, and Jezebel was eaten by Aling Bekang's ginger-furred dog.

When everything was over, Weng-Weng quietly left Aling Bekang. She just woke up one day and found her wooden bed empty, and all his clothes gone from their old closet with no door. She sulked for a week, moped and kept to herself. And then after seven days, she went back to the talipapa, standing at her stall of the brightest heads of squash and the ripest of mangoes.

But when nobody was looking, she would touch the mango's warm and smooth skin, wishing it were a grenade, and wondering when the world would end.

THE HEART OF SUMMER

O n the first day of April, just as summer was about to start, we moved to a row house in a subdivision carved out of the Antipolo mountains.

A row house is a euphemism for a house that somehow managed to fit into a 100-square-metre lot. They looked like matchboxes, really, that were built near the riverbank. The larger houses, of course, stood grandly at the centre of the village, in front of the chapel. We'd be renting the house from the mayor's mistress, one of three houses she owned in the subdivision. It was a small and compact house without divisions, with the living room spilling over to the pantry and the kitchen, and then to the dining area.

The house only had two tiny rooms, but it was enough for us. The owner of the apartment we had been renting in Project 4, Quezon City, wrote to us (in pink stationery with the letterhead 'Dr Antonina Raquiza, PhD') to say that she wanted to raise the monthly rent to 5,000 pesos. If we couldn't agree to her new terms, we'd have two months to vacate. Mama glared at the letter, then said something obscene about our landlady's father. A day later, she began poring over the newspaper ads looking for cheaper rent in the suburbs. Papa's monthly remittances from his engineer's job in Saudi Arabia would not be enough if the landlady were to raise the rent, since he was also sending some nephews and nieces to school. *Noblesse oblige* was what you called it, but it was actually more *oblige* than *noblesse*, as my mother would put it, while slicing garlic and onions in the kitchen, the latter making me shed copious tears once more.

And that was how we moved to the far suburbs of the Antipolo mountains.

It turned out to be a long, hot summer. The days were dull and endless, a desert that seemed to stretch into infinity. During the afternoons, the heat bit into your skin like the thong of a whip. The water in the subdivision's tank began drying up the week after we moved in, so our housemaid, Ludy, and I had to get water from the fire hydrant in the street corner. Even though I hated studying in summer, this time, I actually looked forward to the first day of summer classes at the university, so I could be relieved of this burdensome task.

But since Ludy also went home to Albay that summer (to look for a boyfriend and dance in the *baile* during the fiesta), I had no choice but to do this chore myself. Mama left the house every day for her piano tutorials. I did the laundry and fixed lunch. In the afternoons, I gathered the laundry so easily dried by the oppressive heat up here in the mountains. I folded the clothes and then sorted them out while watching old Nida Blanca and Nestor de Villa cha-cha-chá musicals on television. Sometimes, I would read the beautiful short stories of Estrella Alfon (Ay, *Magnificence!*), or sketch faces on my big, white drawing pad.

I liked to sketch faces when I could tear myself away from my school work and my household chores. It never failed to amaze me how the grey tip of a pencil could make lines that resemble the shape of rain falling, could rise and dip to sketch the outline of a face, go round and round to make a pair of eyes shaped like an almond, or a marble or straight as a sheer line.

Then, in the blue hour before dusk, I would pick up our red plastic pail and walk five houses away to the street corner to get water. I would line up before the wooden carts full of drums, pails and recycled gasoline containers with the upper half sawn off. I carried only a pail, but I was too timid to elbow my way to the head of the line. The short, stocky men nudged each other's ribs and exchanged stories: 'Vodka Banana did it again in her latest, soft-core penetration movie, *Only a Wall Between Us.*'

The women gossiped about their movie idols. 'Sharon's legs are like a laundry woman's paddle,' said one. But she should have looked at herself first, for her varicose veins strained on her legs like netting.

After waiting for almost an hour, I finally reached the fire hydrant. From its open mouth gushed water whose pressure was so strong that it swirled round and round my pail, forming a foam that spilt on the dry, brown earth. Then, I walked back to the house where I carefully poured the water into the drum. And then back to the street corner. Again.

On my way back, darkness had already settled on the hills. The chickens would be roosting on the branches of the star-apple trees and the cicadas would begin their one-note singing. When I reached the street corner again, a young man was standing at the head of the line. He hadn't been there when I left earlier. He must have asked his housemaid to stand in for him and returned only when it was time to fill his drum.

Dusk slept on his rumpled hair. Smooth, nut-brown skin. Eyes, round as marbles. He wore a maroon T-shirt, silk-screened with Mapua College of Engineering, black denim shorts on long legs and brown, leather sandals from Our Tribe.

When he saw me at the end of the line, he walked over to me and said, '*Uy*, you can go ahead, since you only have this pail.' Cool, deep voice.

'Thank you,' I said. Then I smiled at him and followed him to the fire hydrant. I kept stealing surreptitious glances at his hairy legs. When he looked at me, I would shift my attention to the water beginning to fill my pail, swirling round and round, until its foam flowed over the lip of the bucket. I thanked him again, and then gave him my name. He mumbled his name. I smiled, and then walked away. I walked away because I was afraid that any moment now I would tell Richard that I liked him not only because he was considerate, but also because he had such muscular legs and clean toenails.

* * *

That summer, the Bermuda grass in our lawn turned brown. We had hoped for a friendly neighbourhood, similar to the one we had in Project 4, Quezon City, but we were disappointed. A young childless couple lived in the house on the left; both were working, holding down two jobs each like everybody else. We only saw them at Sunday Mass. On the right lived an elderly couple with an only child, a teenage daughter named Mary Belle, who liked to bike around the village in midriff shirts and abbreviated shorts. Her father was a big man with the face of a bulldog, his voice booming across the yard when he barked, er, spoke.

* * *

The minibus station in Cubao slouched on the street right after EDSA (Epifanio de los Santos Avenue). It was housed in a big, abandoned garage. On the hard, earthen floor, the spilt oil looked like lost, black continents on a map.

That summer, I enrolled in two courses: business statistics and financial accounting. I took up business management in this Jesuit university because my father had said it would make us rich. I signed up for the course, although the only thing I wanted to do in the world was to draw. Pencil to paper, lines forming faces. Or sometimes, watercolour to paper, letting the paper soak up the rainbow of colours, forming seas and mountains, the infinity of blue skies.

But I had to go to business school. And so, I left the house at 1 o'clock in the afternoon, after lunch, preferring to take the minibus rather than risk my life in those jeepneys whose deluded drivers thought they were Mad Max. More mad than Max, really.

In the first week of class, I was still adjusting to the hassle of commuting from house to school to house again. It was much easier in Project 4, Quezon City. I would just hop aboard any Cubao-bound bus, get off in front of Queen's Supermarket in the corner of Aurora Boulevard and F. Castillo Street, and then walk all the way home.

But here, I would have to wait for the minibus to fill up with passengers before we could leave. The street would be choked with hawkers selling everything: freshly sliced squash and pointed okra good for a dinner of *pinakbet*, red apples from New Zealand, blue jeans with fake brand names sewn on the back, tabloids with their headlines in red ink blown up to 72 points Times New Roman ('Boa Constrictor in Dept. Store/ Dressing Room Swallows/ Up Female Customers'). Big speakers would boom with rock music from Guns N' Roses, alternating with the syrupy songs of Air Supply. Food stalls offered everything, from cow's entrails floating in lemon-spiked congee to day-old chicks smothered in orange flour, then fried to a crisp brown. And in the air, a cumulus of black exhaust fumes while the dictator, his family, relatives and cronies bled the country dry. Him with his oppressive decrees that passed for the laws of the land; her, with her New York buildings and Monet paintings, her rosaries made of diamonds. And then altogether now, the conjugal dictatorship parcelling the whole country between themselves. Shady deals were drawn for resources in the air (contracts to buy military helicopters and jet fighter planes), land (farms turned to high-end resorts) and water (lakes turned into private fish pens latticed with bamboo fences).

Oh, how I wished I could just flee from all of this. There was nothing here, really, in this city and in this country except a big, black hole that sucked you in and drowned you in its thick ooze of oil. I wished I could go away, but to where? To forestall what W.H. Auden called thoughts of 'elsewhereishness', I just fixed my eyes on the accounting textbook on my lap, even if I could not read by the faint light of the minibus. I was doing this one night and when I raised my face, Richard was just coming in. His white shirt was tucked into his tight jeans. His shirt revealed the curve of his chest. He carried a T-square in one hand and two thick books in the other. His wide forehead was furrowed. Must have had a bad day, I thought, moving to the right side of my seat so I could see him better. I wanted him to sit beside me. I wanted to feel the warmth of his arms and thigh against mine. I wanted so much to ease his discomfort. But a man with halitosis sat beside me instead.

The driver finally came. The engine sputtered and roared, then the vehicle crawled slowly out of the narrow street. Near the street corner, the air became smokier, loud with the cries of hawkers vending barbecued chicken's blood, barbecued chicken's entrails (Intra-Uterine Device), barbecued chicken's feet (Adidas), and barbecued chicken's head (Helmet).

The shrill sound of a policeman's whistle rose above the vendor's cries. At the whistle's cry, the hawkers picked up their wares and then scattered madly in all directions. The charcoal embers left behind glowed eerily in the dark.

* * *

I was sitting in our front yard, admiring my mother's orchids, whose saplings she had asked from friends and which she had nurtured with uncommon care, now fully grown, the leaves shiny, with the texture of skin, and the flowers mottled with magenta and amber, the petals unfurling layer upon layer to the dying afternoon sun.

But as the petals opened, I felt myself entering a forest of limbs. Hair-like seaweeds embraced those limbs. The thighs of the men were smooth like river stones. The V-shapes of their bodies glistened with sweat. Leaves like eyes covered their crotches. But under these leaves lay breathing and beautiful things.

I bolted upright with a start. I looked at the clock. The luminous hands pointed to almost midnight. My back was beaded with sweat, and in the room, there was only unbearable heat. I remained motionless for a while as my dream slipped away, and I was alone, again.

I stepped out of the room and headed for the kitchen. I turned on the light and made myself a cup of rice coffee—toasted rice that was then boiled and brewed into coffee. It was cheap and good for the heart. This was the coffee that my grandmother made in the forest, where they had to flee, during the darkest days of the Japanese Occupation of the Philippines, from 1942-1945.

Cup in hand, I opened the front door. My skin brushed against the dry, brittle air. I sat down on the stairs. The cement was cold. To my left, the skeletal branches of the neighbour's *alibangbang* tree cut the moon into many fragments.

I first smelt rather than heard the coming rain. The sound seemed to come from so far away. It was like a voice calling my name. The sound grew louder and louder by the second. I left the cup on the stair landing, stood up and then ran barefoot in the yard. The whole house, the whole yard, the whole village seemed to be tense, waiting.

Then it quickly came, punching small holes in the night sky, rattling on the roofs, soaking wet both the flowers and the leaves: *Agua de Mayo*! The first rains of May!

In the darkness, the rain's fingers caressed my hair and my face. It began licking my eyelids, earlobes and lips. I opened my mouth and let the rain's tongue roam inside me, while its fingers travelled downward, on my inner arm and my chest. Its lips went around my nipples and navel, kissing my warm, innermost spaces.

Like sunlight, heat rose from the earth, musky heat that entered my soles, warmed my body and then broke out of the pores of my skin. It was brief but it pierced me beautifully, suddenly.

I knew now what I would do. I would soap myself in the bathroom, rinse my skin clean, change into fresh clothes that smelt good and were crisp to touch. Then, I would look for my sheets of Oslo paper in my drawer. I would run my fingers over my sketches of Richard. The rumpled hair and the dark, melancholy eyes. How can I tell him that there is nothing else in the world that I want more than to be with him? Ludy said that Richard would soon join his mother, who was working as a nurse in New York City. So many departures, so few arrivals. But now, I have him; he is here, contained in the purity of my ache.

I would turn off the lights, plunging the house in darkness. Then, I would turn myself over to the arms of sleep. Outside, the leaves would still be moist and breathing.

WINGS OF DESIRE

Like me, my cousin, Ramon, was also the first-born child of my Uncle Conrado and his wife, Emilia.

Papa woke me up early that summer morning. He told me to wash my face because we would go to Manila. My heart skipped with delight, especially when I saw that some of my clothes had already been stuffed in Papa's blue overnight bag.

Papa's eyes were sad. He kissed Mama goodbye, put my grandmother's hand on his forehead, and then we were gone. We took a pedicab to the gate. The young soldier on duty gave my father a crisp salute. Behind him stood the statue of a pilot cast in concrete, his eyes raised to the sky. Soon, we were aboard a jeep bound for the town of Guagua. As usual, the driver manoeuvred the jeep as if he were in the Indianapolis 500. His jeep zipped through the barrio road, the town's main road and finally the highway at the same suicidal speed. Huts and wooden houses, buildings and plantations of sugarcane blurred before us. It always frightened me.

I closed my eyes and dredged my mind for prayers. Miss Honey Joy Tamayo of catechism class said that if you died with a Catholic prayer on your lips, you would go to heaven straight away. So, I began silently reciting the holy rosary, over and over again; the three mysteries repeated for the nth time from the towns of Floridablanca to Guagua, a distance of 20 kilometres, using my fingers to count the Our Fathers, Hail Marys and Glory Bes. If I did not go to heaven, I thought, at least I'd be good in maths.

The driver would suddenly step on the brakes, then rev the engine up, swerve here and there, weaving in and out of our lane, the true king of the road! Above him, a strip of mirror ablaze with decal stickers: *Basta driver; sweet lover; I only rest when I pee.* And directly in front of him, two women. On the left was the decal sticker of a vamp, her overripe body spilling out of her red bikini. The other was the veiled Blessed Virgin Mary, wearing layer upon layer of white clothes, a blue sash wound primly around her waist.

* * *

After forty-five minutes, the jeep swung around the big plaza of Guagua. Then we got off and waited for the big bus bound for Manila. Usually they were air-conditioned Victory Liners, rare in those days, and once we had settled on our seats and paid for the tickets, Papa would begin to sleep, or rather, snore. I would be terribly embarrassed, but nobody seemed to mind, for almost everybody would fall asleep as the morning sun climbed higher in the clear sky of summer.

I would also try to sleep, but from behind my shut eyelids, I could see the tiny, red spots formed by the sunlight. So, I would just open my eyes and watch the world blur past me.

Three big, covered carts, each of which was pulled by a bull, travelled slowly on the shoulder of the road. The carts contained wicker chairs and small tables, mirrors and hammocks, rattan baskets and small shelves. The farmers from the north travelled all over Luzon after the harvest was over and the fields would lie fallow for months. They hoped to sell the hand-crafted things which they had woven and plaited. The carts were framed by billboards advertising the many legendary bounties of the

Philippines: the Banaue Rice Terraces carved into the northern mountains of Ifugao thousands of years ago; Mayon Volcano whose perfect symmetry no eruption could alter; the swift-sailing vintas of Zamboanga; and the Santo Niño of Cebu City, the Christ child capable of performing miracles; everything luring the tourists to the sun, sea and sand, the magic and the mystery, of this calm country with its own brand of a 'smiling martial law'.

The other billboards were from Filoil and B-meg Feeds, Ajinomoto Vetsin and Vitarich, as well as the Mobil gas station with the red, flying horse. But the biggest billboard was the advert showing a gorgeous and fair-skinned hunk in abbreviated white underwear. It was for YC Bikini brief and it was being sold 'for the man who packs a wallop'.

I would check on my father who, by this time, would be in deep sleep. Then I would look outside again, marvelling at the blue dome of the sky. It was rice-planting season again. Rice saplings had just been newly transplanted from their seedbeds, their slim, young leaves stirring in the wind. On the left rose Mount Arayat, a mountain shaped like a stump, gently covered by white, fluffy clouds. The rice fields gave way to the brown, nipa huts alive with the laughter of barefoot children with big bellies. Yellow rice grains left to dry on the sides of the road. White hens with red beaks, cackling. People gathered around the transistor radio with its volume turned up so that everybody could hear other lives endlessly twisting and turning from the morning melodrama, with its narratives of heartbreak and hope. The new wood-and-cement houses built for their parents by young men and women working in the Middle East. The abandoned mansions of the sugar barons, their dry fountains and wide gardens now choked by weeds, the heavy wooden doors now shut. And then the baroque churches, covered with moss and lichen, cratered by wind and rain. And in the air, the heavy, cloying smell of molasses from the mills of the Pampanga Sugar Development Company or PASUDECO, inducing me finally to sleep. Later, this sugar mill would become a big shopping mall, like many of the buildings in the archipelago, grey and air-conditioned boxes filled with colourful things. But today, it was still a sugar mill whose sweet, sweet smell was filling me with such lethargy.

* * *

Manila burst like a bucket of icy water thrown on the face. The Andres Bonifacio Monument loomed (the proletarian hero frozen in a voiceless scream), the bus deftly circling the roundabout, and down we went to Epifanio de los Santos Avenue, the unbearable smell of the Cloverleaf Market, the diesel fumes darkening the air. We got off in a Cubao that still had no shopping malls, just small speciality shops and a row of big cinema houses. Then the jeep ride to the borough of Santa Mesa, so very fast with the miniature steel horses on the hood seemingly clip-clopping in the wind, the thin, plastic strips of many colours flying, the jeep swerving, going up and down a bridge. Then here we were.

My uncle lived in his in-law's house on a strip of government land behind the motels of Old Santa Mesa. *Seven Seas, Heaven Sent, Erotica, Exotica*—I still recall their names in a breathless rush, these places where supposedly illicit love happened between people not married to each other, as my grandmother would say, then she would make her sniff of disapproval. Down we went, down, down the rough steps hewn out of stone. The wooden houses seemed to breathe into each other. One's kitchen ended where another's bedroom began. The alleys coiled round and round like intestines. And when the rainy season came, everything turned muddy, and a perpetual green slime covered the ground for days.

After Papa and I had turned this way and that, poking into someone else's living room and scanning another's open bedroom, we reached the place—a one-storey affair at the foot of the stairs of an old wooden house.

Even at noon, bright lights burnt in the living room. The candelabra's fingers glowed. Under the lights, the coffin of my cousin, Ramon.

My Aunt Emilia broke down at the sight of Papa. '*Manoy*, Mon is gone,' she wailed. 'What will I do?' Sobs tore from her chest, and the old women around her also began to cry like a chorus. They were all in black. Like a flock of crows. Papa let her go on. She blubbered that if only she had known Ramon would sustain a fatal head injury in a basketball game, her son who had been torn out of her by the doctor's forceps . . .

'I shouldn't have allowed him to play in that basketball game. Manoy, should I tell Conrado?'

Silence. Papa seemed to weigh his words very carefully, like stones on a scale. Then, looking straight into my aunt's eyes, actually looking through her, he said, 'I think it would be best not to tell Conrado. I know my brother very well. He'll take it badly. He might . . .' Papa sighed deeply. He suddenly looked tired, and very old. 'He might even jump from the ship if he hears about it.'

My aunt sank silently on to the sofa. She wept wordlessly. It was painful to look at her. I stood up and walked over to the coffin of Ramon.

Atop the glass was his photograph taken a month ago, so very young, his eyes like the clearest water. In his photograph, the gold First Honour medal shone on his white, polo shirt. Leis of white jasmine buds and yellow-green *ylang-ylang* flowers were hung around the photograph. And then, I looked down at him.

* * *

In my dream, my Uncle Conrado has come home. He has left behind him the North Sea, cold enough to break even your bones.

Now he is borne by waves that have slowly shaped themselves into the whitest of wings. The world below is a blue nothingness. The bird glides slowly, reaching an archipelago of the bluest sea and the greenest islands, until it reaches the brown filth that is Manila. The bird alights finally at Old Santa Mesa, and my uncle slides down its feathery body. He waves farewell to the strange, magnificent bird, which nods slowly in acknowledgement. And then, just as suddenly, the bird is gone.

Down, down, down the steps hewn from stone. The air closing in around my uncle, darkness descending, a door opening and closing on its one rusty hinge. *Ramon? Ramon? Where is my son, Ramon?* Words from the palest lips. The electric volt of pain crackling from one nerve ending to another.

Sometimes, when we call out a name, even the very wind crumbles.

A VARIOUS SEASON

This story is for Kerima Polotan

He got off the jeep in front of gate three of the Jesuit university. The monoxide wake of the jeepney trailed him as he walked toward the pavement shrouded with acacias. Here, he breathed in the clean fragrance of a morning after a night of rain. Sunlight leaned against the damp trunks of the trees. He liked to walk here; the wind from Antipolo lightly mussed his hair, unlike in Sampaloc where he lived, with its dry and brittle air.

He wished he had a watch. His classmates had agreed to meet in the lobby of the administration building by seven o' clock in the morning. It would be embarrassing to keep them waiting, he thought. He walked faster.

The soft edges of the building slowly sharpened before his eyes. He knew that he would have to wait for his mother's government-mandated thirteenth-month pay before he could buy a pair of eyeglasses. A white Mercedes-Benz 300 D and a light-blue BMW stood in the parking lot. He gripped the green duffel bag on his shoulders and jogged to the building.

'Hi, Pete, you're just in time,' said Mrs Herrera, rising from the bench to meet him.

'You wore our class shirt, huh?' Pete nodded at her blue T-shirt printed with TOM'S BOYS AND GIRLS in white. Her first name was Tomasita, but they called her Tommie. She just smiled, revealing a set of small and very white teeth.

Pete felt a bead of sweat roll down his temple to the side of his face. He bowed his head, checking if he smelt. Then, he fished out his handkerchief from his pocket and wiped away the sweat.

Beside Tommie stood Mike, her ten-year-old son, whom she sometimes brought to class. 'Pete, you can join Roy, Robert and Carlos in one car. Clark and Mike will ride in my car. Too bad,' she added, shaking her head, 'I really hoped the others could also make it, no?'

'Well, we had better get going, Tommie,' Roy said. He opened the door of the Benz. 'You chose to advise Block Q, the smallest freshman class. Imagine, only twenty freshmen? With only five girls. And then, this outing which is so late. Everybody's already off on their vacation.'

'Okay, let's go,' said Carlos, his delicate cheekbones twitching. I had known him for a year and that was his way of interrupting a conversation that bored him. 'I'm raring to see our resort.' Pete remembered that Carlos's family was a major stockholder in the Seascape Beach Resort and Country Club. He had offered the use of the place. His knit, maroon shirt, with a tiny alligator sewn on the chest, was tucked into stretch jeans. He wore brown penny loafers over argyle socks.

The group got into their respective cars. Carlos sat beside Pete at the back, placing his white Puma bag between them. Pete picked up his duffel bag and put it on his lap.

'Okay, Robert?' asked Roy, putting on his sunglasses whose French brand name Pete could barely pronounce.

'Sure,' answered Robert.

'Hang on, guys!' said Roy. He pulled out of the parking lot, trailing Tommie's BMW which she drove herself. The coldness of the car began to seep into Pete's skin.

* * *

In his first year at the university, Pete tried to associate with his classmates, most of them scions of the rich, their English as smooth as their expensive and well-pressed clothes. He had been lucky, indeed, to get a scholarship to this exclusive university. Otherwise, he would have studied in one of the diploma mills in the university belt, the only schools his mother could afford. His engineer-father, a large, laughing man who did not believe in exigencies such as savings and insurance, had died in a jeepney accident when Pete was only ten years old. With raw bitterness, Pete often thought that his father had left them nothing, only a small house amongst a row of skinny houses in a potholed street. Since then, his mother had been bringing up four children on a teacher's miserable salary. She also moonlighted as a memorial-park agent and sold dresses from the town of Cainta to her co-teachers.

He had talked to her two days ago. 'Ma, this beach party will also be our farewell party for Tommie, our teacher. She'll emigrate to Canada next month. Besides, she'll pay for my expenses, my birthday gift from her. Also, Ma, my grades will keep me in the Dean's List this sem. I can also practise the swimming styles I had learnt at the Young Men's Christian Association last summer,' he said, silently congratulating himself, because he had marshalled his reasons neatly.

'All right, all right, you may go,' she answered, 'but since it's your birthday tomorrow, promise me that you won't swim. Promise me, Pete.'

Couldn't I swim just in the shallow area? he had wanted to ask. But he knew she would not budge. She looked frail on the outside, head usually bowed when she walked, but inside she was tough. Like a mung seed, she could be left anywhere, and she would survive. He wanted to dismiss her argument as a mere superstition; he believed one met with an accident, or even died, if fated to meet with an accident or die on that day, whether it was your birthday or not.

But her large, black eyes were tired. The lipstick had gone grainy in the tiny grooves on her lips. 'Okay, Ma, I promise,' he had said, gravely. 'Ma,' he began again, this time in a cheerful tone, 'can we have my birthday party on Sunday evening after I arrive from Bataan? My party with you, Dino, James and Jenny, huh?' Her face bloomed into a smile, her eyes lighting up. Pete checked the impulse to touch her face, ashamed of his sudden tenderness.

The Benz stopped with a sudden lurch. They had nearly side-swiped a tricycle. Through the tinted windshield, the old driver's face looked cracked. His hair was ashen. He was too stunned to react, frozen on the battered, black seat of the motorcycle. There was something vaguely familiar about him, but Pete brushed the thought aside. Around them, the sun-roasted stalls were filled with watermelons, mangoes, fish, meat and leafy vegetables. He breathed in the air inside the Benz, cleansed of the stink that he knew hung about the open-air market. Carlos hissed *shit!* loudly. He pushed his gold-framed eyeglasses up over his nose, a nose shaped like a parrot's beak. Then, his pale fingers slid down to touch a small and fresh pimple throbbing beneath his lips.

Roy was about to open the door. But Robert touched Roy's shoulder. 'Hey, that's nothing. Nobody's hurt. Why do you have to bother about it?'

Roy's face darkened with annoyance. 'What if my car was scratched?' he asked sharply.

Robert shook his head, then fingered his scraggly moustache. He had been the president of Block Q, a tall, muscle-bound guy who spoke with the usual nasal accent. During the first days of classes, everybody had been wary of a classmate from outside the clique: the five girls from the schools run by Catholic nuns stayed in the middle of the room, sandwiched between the boys from the two rival Catholic schools. Pete was the only scholar in the class. But Robert talked to him, always reminding him to be careful, saying that the city is different, ending his talk with brotherly taps on Pete's shoulders.

Now, it occurred to Pete that his Big Brother had thought all along that he had come from the province. In the swiftly moving car, he realized it must have been his clothes—usually a plain white T-shirt, faded jeans and rubber shoes—and the crude way he spoke English, at a loss for the proper and elegant enunciation, which led Robert to presume. In spite of the cool air, blood rushed to Pete's head. It took him a few minutes to calm down, helped along by the car's frigid air. I won't waste time with this, he told himself, I just want to enjoy the beach party.

'Fasten your seat belts, guys!' Roy said aloud when they reached the North Expressway. The speedometer's needle began to move to the right, pointing to 100. Roy turned on the radio to full volume; the clash of metal blasted in their ears. Robert lit up a joint. A strange sweetish smoke floated above them. Robert passed on the stick to Carlos.

'Hey, don't forget me!' Roy shouted. His voice cut through the twang of the electric guitars. Carlos gave the joint to Roy, who took a deep drag at it. They know I don't take it, Pete said in silence, reassuring himself why he was conveniently ignored. He just leaned back on the soft, black upholstery of the car, looking at the countryside sweeping past them, a lattice of rice fields with the greenest leaves, as far as the eye could see.

* * *

The morning sun had not yet erased the mist hovering over the sea. The breeze turned the feathery cogon flowers on the roadside into rippling, white waves. Grey, two-storeyed buildings, with grilled, mother-of-pearl windows and brick-tiled roofs, had been built at the foot of the hills. A group of cabanas were clustered together like colourful petals around the blue swimming pools. The Benz stopped under a canopy of tall coconut trees. The sky was barely visible through the palm leaves interlacing overhead.

'We're here!' Carlos said with glee. He pulled out his Puma bag that had stood between him and Pete like a low wall. Outside the car, Pete checked the impulse to brush his clothes and comb his hair with his fingers. He heard the faint hum of cement mixers and the growl of bulldozers. It must be the construction of the townhouses in the hills, he thought, remembering the steel bars on the earth that they had seen, while they rounded the bend near the resort.

Still feeling sticky despite the cool ride, Pete decided to take a bath. He went directly to the shower stalls. He took off his clothes but was suddenly alarmed. He did not know which knob was for the hot or cold water, and whether to push or pull it. The toilet and bath had been crammed together in their small house. In that badly lit room, he used a tin can to draw water from an old steel drum. Sometimes, no water would flow from the tap. He would walk to the end of the street, a pail in hand, and pump water from the rusty artesian well. Cracks yawned on the floor of their bathroom, but not even a single chipped tile had been put on their walls. But in this stall, flooded with light, the blue-and-white tiles had been arranged to form small rectangles on the walls. He pulled the stainless-steel knob on the right side, and cold water rained down on him.

After dining on chicken a la Kiev, boiled prawns dipped in melted butter, tossed green salad and fresh fruits with scoops of vanilla ice cream, they gathered around the bonfire on the beach.

'C'mon, let's sing a "Happy Birthday" for Pete,' Mrs Herrera suggested. The light from the bonfire gleamed in her eyes.

'Okay, I'll sing,' Clark Kent Co volunteered, his left hand on the neck of a Remy Martin cognac. A Chinese character, which he had said stood for love, was printed in white on his black cotton shirt. His face was already ruddy.

'Oy, Superman, let's all sing, okay?' Robert asked, 'O, one, two, three . . .' They all sang for Pete. Catcalls erupted when a voice wandered out of tune.

'Thanks,' Pete murmured. The warmth of the fire reached his face: a strange buoyancy flowed in his veins. He had meant to suggest a walk on the beach, but his tonsils suddenly began to itch. He cleared his throat, as if it would drive away the itch. But it did not. He could feel a clot forming in his throat. 'Tommie,' he began tentatively, 'I . . . think I'll go directly to my room. My tonsils are getting itchy again.' He spoke in the same manner and tone he used during the first day of class; his classmates had all graduated from schools run by religious orders, and when it was his turn to speak, he had mumbled the name of his government high school.

'Go ahead, Pete. Mike also has a cold because it rained heavily last night. We'll also go up in a few minutes. Take care. Good night.'

'Good night to you, too,' he replied, wishing Robert, Roy, Clark and Carlos would answer. But they had begun talking loudly amongst themselves.

Pete walked away. The strong wind carried to him the drift of their conversation: 'Seen the new Audi?' . . . 'Volvo better? . . . 'Benz is still the best' . . .

His room was next to the stair landing. He turned on the light. I've long wanted a room all my own, he thought, as he walked inside. But they only had two rooms in their house. Sometimes, he was annoyed by the sight of them, three brothers crowded in a small room, sleeping on a mat unrolled on the cold floor. His sister slept in the room of his mother.

After turning off the lights, he lay on the bed whose soft mattress sank under him. He tried to sleep, but he could not. I somehow miss the mat that I share with Dino and Gerry, he chuckled to himself. He pieced together the things that had happened during the day, a trick that never failed to put him into sleep. But after what seemed like an hour, he was still awake. The itch in his throat had become sharper and now, his throat was beginning to burn. He jumped out of bed and fumbled for his slippers in the dark. He opened the door and ran to the washroom.

He examined his throat in the mirror. His tonsils had swollen. The red, pulp-like tissue was now aflame. It must have been the three scoops of vanilla ice cream he had eaten earlier. He dreaded his tonsillitis because it always came with chills and fever, then left him with a cough sounding like a guttural bark. Suddenly, he felt helpless and alone; he wished he were home. At the first sign of his tonsillitis, his mother would rush to their room. She would scold him lightly for taking cold soft drinks and letting the sweat dry on him. But immediately afterwards, her rituals would begin: she would pop the antibiotic Ospen into his mouth. Then, she would wash it down with the lukewarm *calamansi* juice that Dino had earlier prepared for him, the tartness of the small lemons making him wince, and rub Vicks VapoRub on the skin near his nostrils. Then, she would massage his temples. And after she had finished rubbing the ointment on his neck, chest and back, he would feel relaxed, the tide of pain beginning to subside in his throat. Jenny would hover around the bed, giving him a moist kiss on the cheek despite his protests that she might catch his fever. Then, he would sink into a deep and relaxed sleep.

But now, chills tore his body. He shivered, then took several deep breaths. Slowly, he walked out of the washroom. He stopped before Mrs Herrera's room and knocked softly. Then, he leaned his body against the wall.

'Mike has fever!' Her words spilt out in a rush even before she had fully opened the door. Her eyes seemed older. The lipstick had gone grainy on the tiny grooves of her lips. Pete thought of his mother. 'I've given him an Aspilet. He's now sleeping.'

He didn't want to worry her further, but he had chills. His fingers dug at the wall for support. 'Did you bring any antibiotics with you?' He spoke slowly, because every word seemed to slash his throat. A gust of cold wind swept in from the sea.

'Oh God, you have a fever as well!' she exclaimed, touching his neck. 'Sit inside. I'll go back to the car. I think I still have some Ampicin there somewhere.'

He sat on the edge of the chair, outside the arc of gold cast by the lamp. Mike slept soundly, snuggled like a kitten on the bed. Pete doubled up, hugging his knees, when chills tore his body again. Crazily, he wished for a magic carpet outside the door so he would be back home in a few seconds. His body was drenched in sweat. Pain drilled down his throat. The dark hovered over him, its breath like a shadow . . .

* * *

He woke up with a start. Someone was knocking on the door. The morning light pressing against the shell-pane windows brought a strange radiance into his room. He stood up, flexing his arms again and again, like a butterfly with wet wings just emerging from a cocoon.

'Hi!' Mrs Herrera greeted him warmly as he opened the door. Her eyes glistened, alive again. 'You were already sleeping when I returned. You're lucky that I found Ampicin in the car.'

'Where is it?'

'Hey, you've already taken one last night, remember? I woke you up and gave you one, then I walked you to your room,' she said, brightly. 'Here, you may take another capsule.' She handed him the tinfoil-wrapped pill.

Suddenly, he remembered a warm hand shaking him awake in the dark and popping a capsule into his mouth. Instinctively, he had waited for the lukewarm calamansi juice, but his tongue had only tasted the flatness of tap water.

Their breakfast of bacon, scrambled eggs, white bread, red watermelons and hot, thick chocolate was already laid on the table when Pete walked into the dining hall. The hall was empty, except for their group.

It was hard for him to swallow. At home, when he was ill, his mother would prepare congee and boiled native chicken's eggs for his breakfast.

After breakfast, his classmates all stood up to a man. 'Ooooops!' Mrs Herrera said, 'Changing to your trunks again, huh? Can't you wait another hour?'

'We'll swim only in the shallow area, Mrs Girl Scout,' Roy said in jest.

'Do you want to join us, Pete?' Clark asked.

'Aaaaah,' he answered.

'He'll join you maybe later, right, Pete?' suggested Mrs Herrera. Pete nodded.

After his classmates had all left, Pete fumbled for words. Mrs Herrera and Mike sat opposite him, sipping their chocolate soundlessly. Pete cleared his throat and finally spoke. 'I'll go ahead, Tommie. I'll look around for cowrie shells for my sister.'

'Are you sure you're okay?'

'Yes, I'm fine. And thanks,' he said.

He still felt weak around the limbs but thought some walking would not harm him. In the sun-drenched morning, he relaxed as the breeze touched his skin. He inhaled the breeze redolent with the tang of salt. The waves hummed. The sand was beginning to get warm as he walked barefoot. He looked down and followed the trails of hermit crabs, bending now and then to pick up cowrie shells that he collected in the front pockets of his jeans.

Good, he thought, that Tommie didn't mention to the guys that I had been terribly ill. Telling them would only invite 'Oh, yeahs?'

He stopped before the bonfire that had burnt intensely the night before, the flame flowering in the dark. Now, only a pile of cindered ash remained.

He sat on a coconut log that had been painted white. The roof of his mouth was turning rigid again; he was recovering. He smiled, remembering the food that his mother never failed to prepare for everyone's birthday.

'*Pancit Canton* noodles and purple-yam ice cream again?' they would snicker.

His mother would counter: 'Jenny likes the ice cream; Dino and James like the Pancit Canton noodles; and you,' she would lift her chin because he was five inches taller than her, 'you like both!' His brothers and sister would break into laughter, warm and rich, floating like candle-glow about them.

Voices suddenly splintered his thoughts, carried by the wind rising from the sea. He turned around and saw his classmates in their expensive swimming trunks, racing to the water. Robert and Clark swam towards a hut on a bamboo raft near the shore. Clark hoisted himself on to the raft when he reached it first; droplets of water ran down his body. From where he sat, Pete could see Clark enjoying himself immensely, his laughter crackling in the bright morning air. He waved at Pete, who just ignored him.

Pete walked away, thinking of the word he had given his mother, although he wanted to show them how well he swam. He walked aimlessly and soon found himself in front of the big resort office. He opened the glass-panelled door. The air-conditioner hummed. On the walls bloomed posters in soft-lens photography. The glossy posters sang of the facilities in Seascape Beach Resort and Country Club *(where one is in rich company)*: fifty furnished rooms, two Olympic-sized swimming pools, tennis courts, 100 first-class townhouses . . . His fingertip ran down one shiny page of the brochure; one townhouse cost more than his mother's salary in her remaining twenty years as a teacher. Even the money she would earn selling memorial-park lots and dresses from Cainta would never be enough.

He left the office in haste. Outside, a young, dark-skinned worker was pushing a wheelbarrow, rushing to the hills where the townhouses waited to be finished. Suddenly, Pete remembered another young, dark-skinned worker whom they had seen the day before. They had been standing on the terrace, feasting on pork barbeque and beer. Mrs Herrera and Mike were in their room, so Robert was free to brag about the 'fantastic techniques' of his American girlfriend in San Francisco where he had gone to high school. From nowhere, the young, dark-skinned worker stopped before them, a bundle of firewood in the crook of his left arm. He wore faded jeans with holes, his earth-brown body in a Citizen's Military Training uniform that he must have worn in a government high school. He had matted, shoulder-length hair; sweat glistened on his face. He looked as if he had come from a faraway place. After nodding politely at Carlos, he spoke softly in the native language. '*Señorito*, I was told to make a bonfire . . .'

'Good, make it fast!' Carlos snapped, his delicate cheekbones twitching again. Later, he said that the worker was one of the tenants of the vast Lopez rice estate in Nueva Ecija who had been brought here to finish the construction of the townhouses. After seeing the fire, Carlos waved the worker away. The worker just bowed in silence, but when he raised his face, something like a shard glinted in his eyes. But it shone only briefly, for soon, he had turned away and vanished into the dusk.

Now, inside his room, something stirred inside Pete. He felt a sudden ache as a face began to form in his mind, the cracked face of an old man with ashen hair. He remembered that the old tricycle driver yesterday looked like his dead grandfather, a miner in the province of Masbate in the Bicol Region before the Second World War. The old man's face and features were frozen in the sepia photographs that Pete's mother had kept in the wooden trunk. It dawned on Pete that his skin was dark brown, so much like the earth in which his grandfather had mined for gold; and his palms were coarse, so much like his grandfather's, gripping the wooden handle of a pick in that photograph taken in another time. But now, Pete was amongst the owners of the gold mines and the vast estates of rice, owners of this elegant resort and the expensive townhouses, rising bone-white beneath the sun.

When he reached the terrace, his classmates were still horsing around in the water. He looked at the shimmer of the sea beyond the shallow spot where his classmates swam. The radiance cupped by the sea seemed bright enough, reminding him of scenes from his home: eating corn on the cob dripping with Star margarine because they had no butter that day when Tropical Cyclone Asyang tore through the city; his mother telling them outrageous tales about his large, laughing father, changing an event here or a punchline there with each retelling; Jenny, Dino and James dancing the rock lobster and laughing; something floating about them, warm and rich, like candle-glow . . .

He stood quietly, looking blankly ahead, when his classmates' voices drifted from the shore. In his mind's eye, they rose ghostly pale from the sea, separated from him in this season of summer. Their voices tried to splinter his thoughts again, but the wall between them now seemed thick and impenetrable.

LETTER TO BRIAN

10 September 19xx

My dearest Brian,

I'm glad that you're with me on your birthday. From my writing table I see you lying in my bed. Your back is turned to me and you're shirtless. You're still sound asleep, unmindful of the light streaming in from the open window on to your face.

Ah, your face.

I was going upstairs to the second floor of the café, and as before, I was dragging my feet again. My friends tell me that when I walk, I seem to be dragging everything. When I turned to the left, I saw you, sitting there, all alone. Your very fine hair cascaded down over your forehead. I noticed your eyes first. You have the saddest eyes I've ever seen.

I talked to you. We became friends, we watched films, we made love. And now, one month after I first met you, one day after your twenty-fifth birthday, you're sleeping in my bed while I watch you. You told me last night, while we were having dinner by candlelight (we weren't romantic, it was just that last night there was a blackout again), you told me that you're happy.

You said, 'When I opened the door of your flat you were there, and you embraced me tightly.'

And I told you, while we were lying in bed, our hands clasped: 'I'm sorry, Brian. I can't give you anything else on your birthday. All my jewellery is made of brass and cheap silver from Baguio City.'

Then, I suddenly remembered Baguio: jogging during early morning while the cold set one's teeth on edge, the tall pine trees shrouded with mist and the soft light of the sun. 'Let's go to Baguio in December, if we have money,' I suggested, kissing your hair.

You answered me with an embrace. You kissed my face gently, my ears and the slope of my neck. Our naked bodies grew warmer. Our hands played, talked to each other in a language only they could understand. And then we began to float . . .

A while ago, we had a simple birthday dinner: fried chicken and noodles from Max's which I had bought immediately after my classes at the university. Noodles, of course, for long life. We ate in silence. The candlelight fell softly on our faces, our skin. Our hearts were full.

After eating and clearing away the dishes, we sat on the sofa. And then you told me your story. Black is the thread of life, and it's knotted tightly inside your chest.

'My father left my mother when he knew she was already pregnant. My aunt adopted me, but she herself was poor. She had only studied up to her grade I. She didn't know any other way to earn a living. I don't know whether I should tell you these things, but it's better that you know where I come from.' I squeezed his hand, nodding all the while.

'She became the mistress of a Chinese merchant in Ongpin. Sometimes, he would beat her. When she could not take it any longer, she ran away. She went to Rizal Park, alone and penniless. As night fell, she met a woman who seemed nice enough. But she turned out to be a mama-san. She brought my adoptive mother to the *casa* and forced her into sex work. And then—' you broke off. Even without looking at you, I know your face is already glistening with tears. I felt as if my skin was being cut by a knife, so very fine and sharp. I quickly wiped away your tears.

'After the mama-san died, my adoptive mother took over the job. And then one fine day, a man fell in love with my mother. He became her boyfriend. He gave me my surname. He stayed with us while my mother continued working in the casa. He was from Pampanga and he was a good cook. His speciality was *sisig*, the cheeks and ears of a pig sliced to small pieces and fried in onions and other condiments. Every time we would eat, he would tell me, "*Mangan tana*. Let us eat." He seemed kind enough, but sometimes, he would kick me when he was drunk.

'He died of cirrhosis of the liver, but before he died, I remember him saying something. We were standing around his hospital bed when he said to my mother: "Please take care of Brian." And because of that I will always remember him with gratitude and affection, even if he used to kick me.'

I stood up, opened the refrigerator, and got out some beers for us. The bottles were very cold and I gripped them tightly.

'My second stepfather headed the security force in a newspaper. He brought us to his house in Santa Cruz and told my mother to stop being a mama-san. He even sent me to a private Catholic school. For years they had no child. They thought my mother could no longer have children.

'My new stepfather was also very cruel. One day, when I was in grade II, he fetched me from school. He was walking beside me, taking me down an unfamiliar road, and then he led me astray. When I turned to look at him, he had already vanished. I was very young, and I didn't know the way home. I walked and walked, until I saw the familiar posts and houses, landmarks which I had memorized on the way home. Even though my mother was furious, she couldn't do anything about this.

'After I finished grade school, I overheard my stepfather telling my mother, "We should send him to a public high school this time. Anyway, he's not your own son, he's merely adopted—and you're already pregnant with our child.' Months later, Alex was born. He grew up to be a tall and good-looking boy. All the family's attention was focused on him. They ignored me again.'

Silence. You took a swig from the bottle of San Miguel beer.

'Everything revolved around Alex. I began to rebel. I cut classes. I just walked around the city: first at Avenida Rizal, then in the district of Quiapo and finally, at Plaza Lawton. Later on, I would roam around Malate and Sucat, even all the way to Las Piñas. My mother would spank me. One time, she slapped me with her wooden clogs until blood spurted from my lips. Another time, she was so mad she thrashed me on the back with a chair, over and over again, until the chair splintered and broke . . . I only went to school once or twice a week. But when I did attend classes, I did my best to catch up with the lessons I had missed. But it was hard. I thought I would never be able to finish high school, but I did.

'After high school, I enrolled in mass communication at the City University of Manila. I wanted to be a journalist. But my rebellion continued. My mother took very good care of Alex. They bought him the toys and clothes which I never had. When I was home, I had to help my mother with the household chores, while Alex grew up like a prince. He just played with his toys and waited to be called for lunch or dinner.

'After one semester, I failed my humanities subject. My teacher talked to me on the last day of class. She said, "Brian, you're not dumb, you know that. You could have passed my subject if you didn't skip classes all the time." I was silent. She wrote to my parents.

'One night, I overheard my parents talking again. My stepfather said, "He should stop his studies. He just keeps loafing around. Anyway, he's merely an adopted child, not our own son."

'Adopted. It's just one word, but it recalls such deep and terrible wounds. That word summarizes everything I do not have. And because my stepfather provided for us, my mother was silent again. She did not even defend me . . .

'I eventually left home. I stayed with relatives in the slums. I worked as a dishwasher in a restaurant. When I could overhear my relatives beginning to complain, I left again. I felt as if I were slowly beginning to vaporize. One day, when I was having a haircut, the gay beauty-parlour attendant, Remy, asked me to stay with him. I did. Remy was kind. He took care of me, but at night he would blow me. I could not do anything. I also liked what he was doing. I began to admit to myself that I liked gays, especially those who are soft, those who look like women. This is better, I said to myself that first night Remy was pulling down my underwear, this is better than working as a construction worker and getting sun-burnt; this is better than pounding the streets of the city looking for work that paid a pittance.

'One day, I met a gay showbiz reporter in Remy's parlour. We were talking when he suddenly said, "You know, you've got some brains. Do you want to write for a showbiz magazine?" I smiled. Why not? I said "yes". The wages may have been small, but it was better than nothing. And so, I interviewed the beautiful but dumb film stars. I would embroider their words in my article, adding this quote and that line, giving depth and dimension to these stars. I wrote about the Dimples King, so-called because he had a dimpled arse. I also wrote about the Hair King, because he had such luxuriant pubic hair.

'My editor liked my writing. He gave me a lot of assignments until one day, I met a rising movie director. He was kind. He taught me how to look at the camera, how to light a scene. He brought me to his home so I could watch his tapes of beautiful films; he used to teach at an exclusive Catholic school.

'He considered me his student, his protégé. We would watch a film ten, twenty times, then he would quiz me about the blocking of the actors, the editing, the production design. He lent me his books on the cinema. He taught me one thing: to look at the light and shadow of things.

'In his house I watched the films of Akira Kurosawa. How could I forget how the rain fell in *The Seven Samurai*? In his house, I watched *Cinema Paradiso*. How could I forget Toto, who so loved the cinema? Like him, I, too, had lost a father. All his life he longed for somebody who would love him. He carried this pain until the very end of the film.

'One day, the director told me, "You know, you have depth. You can be a good director. I will hire you as an assistant for my next film." But before he could hire me, his last film flopped at the box office. Mother Tiger, the producer, was so mad. She also didn't like the fact that he was the only director in her employ who had the nerve to answer her back. She dropped him, and he returned to teaching.'

I was suddenly quiet, and you asked me why. Then you smiled at me. 'Why,' you asked, 'are you jealous? There was nothing between the director and me. You know, one time when the director and I were talking, he admitted to me that he, too, was gay. But he was not in any relationship. He seemed afraid, or just plain hesitant. It must have been a generational problem. We listed the actors we liked. The director and I, we looked so tough, so butch.'

'Macho gays,' I said, rising suddenly. I went to the refrigerator, opened it and got out the left-over chicken. I re-heated it and then served it on the table. 'O, finger food, Mr Butch,' I said. You came over to me, played with my hair and then embraced me.

You said, 'Only now have I met somebody like you. Intelligent, kind, good-looking. You're so different from me. One night, when I could not sleep, I wrote a story. I called it "The Acacia Tree and the Earth". The earth is so grateful that even though he is so low and dirty, the acacia tree has decided to give him a cool and generous shade.'

I looked into your eyes. 'Why do you have such low self-esteem? I don't care who you are or where you came from. I would also do all the things you did if I had to. I don't like to judge or condemn. And you know, the acacia tree won't live, won't have leaves and flowers, if the earth doesn't give it sustenance.'

'You're really quick,' you said. 'That's one more thing I like about you.'

'And pray tell, where else can you find somebody like me? You know what my friends call me? MMMM. Model Melanie Marquez in Megamall. Melanie Marquez won as Miss International and was the first runner-up at the Ford Global Search for Models. That megamall is like a long, fashion ramp for me. I love walking there, especially on the megamall's upper levels, away from all the trying-hard people. My friends and I walk there in our short shorts, shocking everybody.'

He suddenly said, 'I hope you won't abandon me the way my parents did.'

I took a deep breath. 'Let's give it a try, Brian. We should take it a day at a time. I can't promise forever. All I know is that I love you very much. The German poet, Rainer Maria Rilke, said that lovers are two people who used to be one, but now they're together again and looking at the same horizon—the point where the sea and the sky meet.'

And now we are one again. Your fine hair falls on my chest, slowly, like silent water. And our two bodies are one again. Our breaths are ragged and hot. We almost set the whole room ablaze.

The world had turned.

Tomorrow, I would go to work again. One of my dearest friends and colleagues at the office asked me, 'Hey, why is there a glow in your face? You're like a light bulb!'

'He must be in love,' said a younger employee. I just laughed at them.

There must be a light shining from somewhere deep within me. My hands will shield this candle flame. I will take care of it. No winds, no sorrows, could smite it.

I knew that you are now in your mother's house, Brian, while the rain falls on the roof and everybody has already gone to sleep. The rain falls like so many lines in your favourite film, *The Seven Samurai*. You're writing a new film script, catching the light and shadow of things.

We would see each other again on Saturday. We would watch *The Crying Game* at the Megamall. Neil Jordan wrote good stories, but I had not yet seen any of his films. You would again explain to me the scenes: what cameras were used, the shots, the lighting. The people around us would be annoyed with your side comments, and they would all move away. I would whisper to you to turn down the volume of your voice.

You would lower your voice. You would hold my hand, raise my thigh and let it rest on top of your leg. We would watch this film that wove a lovely tapestry of our lives while at the back of the cinema, stand the shadows—gays who were looking for light and warmth in a world dark and cold.

After the film, we would go home and eat the chicken *adobo* I had prepared. I was not a very good cook, I didn't know how to cut the chicken into pieces, but everything could be learnt (ah, the wonderful smell of adobo filling our small kitchen!). After dinner, we would sit on the sofa, very close to each other.

And as I promised, it would be my turn to tell my stories. We would only know each other if we opened the windows and doors inside us.

* * *

But like many love stories, this also ended way too soon. Brian was very self-centred. His navel was his world. One day, he came home and found me listening to Bach. He said it sounded like funeral music and that I should stop listening to it. Of course, I just ignored him and kept on listening to Bach.

Another time, he complained that my friends looked down on him because he was poor. I told him to just ignore my friends. But he kept on needling me about it and even tried to stop me from going to my friends' birthday parties.

'You will just have a good time in the houses of your rich friends, while I stay here in our cramped condominium unit, eating leftovers,' he complained to me one day. It took all of my self-control not to burst into my notorious Aries temper. But the next time he forbade me from attending my rich friends' parties, I just left the house and slammed the door behind me.

Small things, little things, like drops of water destroying the solidity of a rock.

Then one day, he just decided to stop having sex with me. He said, 'Too much sex is not good in any relationship.'

I wanted to ask him, 'Have you counted the number of times we made love in one year?' But I stopped myself since, as I said, I wasn't too good at maths. He just turned his back on me every night we slept beside each other. He began to snore within ten minutes.

One evening, he brought home a young and good-looking man. The young man was polite, but he looked at me with a sly smile on his face.

'This is Roland,' Brian said. 'I brought him here so you can have sex with him. In this way, you won't have to go out and look for it in so many different places.'

I drew Brian aside and fought with him. 'So, you think I'm having sex left, right and centre with other people?'

'Maybe . . . I don't know. That's why I just hired someone for you. This stud is supposedly good. He will make you very happy.'

My blood suddenly boiled over and my temper flared. My fist turned into a ball that swung at his chin with a deadly aim. He fell against the stove and the young man, Roland, stopped me from punching Brian again. I grabbed my bag and stormed out of the condominium unit.

And that was the last time I saw Brian, who swore that he would love me forever.

So much for words. They have always been as fragile as a garden filled with the whorls of flowers and iridescent butterflies' wings. The petals of various colours toss in the wind, as soft and smooth as the face of one's beloved that one cups in one's hand. The butterflies are either floating in the still air or sipping the nectar of flowers as sweet as a lover's promises. Aye, those words.

They never meant anything at all.

THE COUNTRY OF DESIRE

My real name is Juan, which is actually a generic name in my Latin Asian country, which spent 300 years in a Spanish convent and fifty years in Hollywood. It would seem as if my parents had no imagination at all. They didn't even name me after the Catholic saint of the day that I was born, as was the wont of their elders. I guess they wanted to be modern. So, I just called myself 'Jon'. It isn't pronounced 'Jan', which is American, but 'Jon'. Veddy British, the way I liked it.

When the British colonized the Philippines in 1762, they should have stayed for more than two years. If they had, the colonizers would have been as trade-based as the Spaniards, but they would have taught us English as well. And British English at that, not this version that we now call Taglish, for Tagalog English. Or Engalog for English Tagalog. Whatever.

Because even though I was still very young, I already knew that the British were more elegant and sophisticated than the Americans. The Old World was always better than the New World, class versus crass. The British also had Her Majesty the Queen, Queen Mary, even if her children looked like horses.

The Americans, they only had first ladies who were also crystal gazers. Remember Nancy Reagan? She was just a slimmer and older version of our crystal gazers and clairvoyants who plied their trade outside Quiapo Church, in deepest, darkest Manila.

But how did I know that Queen Mary's children looked like horses? Well, I actually saw them. Not just in pictures, as many people did, but in real, living colour. When I was doing research at the uni in Stirling, I was at the library when I heard a public announcement that everyone should now leave the library. Princess Marionette, the queen's daughter, was visiting to give funds for a research grant to the uni or something.

But I was then doing research about a paper on the poetry of the Second World War in Great Britain (I liked the theatres of war and other disturbances), that was why I didn't leave the library. After one hour, driven by pangs of hunger, I stood up from my library carrel and began picking up my books. I was walking down the light-green carpeted stairs when I met someone coming up. Her cold, blue eyes were directed at me, her head tilted to the right. As if she was waiting for me to greet her or to curtsey. Her pink suit was lovely and tailored well, and the way they had teased her hair was not bad at all. But the face?

I suddenly remembered my father, who was a devoted habitué of the horse races at the Saint Lazarus hippodrome.

I did not curtsey; I did not even bow before her. I just looked through her, the way she did to me. She should first ask someone to trim her long chin. It looked like the half-moon chin of the daughter of a controversial politician, the one who said, 'He refused to die.' But he ultimately did die, the poor sod, another dictator bloated beyond belief by lupus erythematosus, a disease in his kidney that ate away at his insides and later drained the colour from his face, making him look like a mask made of ash. Like a whole archipelago taking revenge on the body politic.

And then I continued walking down the stairs. Down there I met a swarm of Princess Marionette's security detail. Now that was a dream: the Englishmen generally looked better than their women, suave in their dark suits, the cool fabrics trying to contain the bulge of a muscle and the strain of something else.

I am Jon. I always rushed headlong—and heedlessly—through life.

But even if I fancied myself as a rebellious teenager, I did follow everything that my parents taught me when I was young. I folded my blanket, plumped my pillows and flattened my bedsheet every morning that God had made. I always sat at the breakfast table with my face already washed, my teeth, brushed and my mouth, gargled. I knew how to use cutlery even at a young age and I cheerfully ate the breakfast of sweet hotdogs and sunny-side-up eggs, with the sides slightly burnt, the way I would always like it.

My father was a corporate lawyer. Like me, he also liked the theatres of war and other disturbances, but these he fought in the expensive board rooms. He liked us to be clean in face and clothing the moment we sat down to eat. And the posture should be as straight as a ruler. I guess he got this training from my grandfather, who had been a general during the hallucinogenic days of the military dictatorship.

So, I straightened my posture, studied hard from grade school to the uni, and prayed the Hail Mary every day before I went to sleep. My father's smile was always brighter than the day every time he attended my graduation ceremonies. I didn't get just one or two medals. Ma'am, I harvested them. I wasn't just the first-honours student; I was also the best in English, the best in social studies, the best in deportment and the best in community service.

The medal in English was easy to get. I'd been reading encyclopaedias since I was young, a complete set of the *Encyclopaedia Britannica* that my grandfather, the general, gave to my father. I read everything, from *Aardvark* to *Zygote*. I concentrated on the British writers, from the entries on Sir Gawain of the Green Knight down to Graham Greene. I also avidly read the pages on the theatre of the war, where the British pillaged countries during their colonizing moments, and later fought alongside the United States to save the Free World from the clutches of the communists.

The medal for the best in deportment (or the most well-behaved), was also a breeze to get. I just didn't show to them my sharp elbows and my even sharper tongue. As I was growing up, I believed more and more in the dictum that 'perception is everything' as the former first lady would put it. She used to be a B-movie star, who would later hoard Monets and Manets using billions stolen from public funds. Like another character from a Latin American banana republic.

But I just behaved very well indeed when I was young. I was a deeply closeted Catholic in a conservative country that was not yet in the twentieth century. People like me didn't exist, for even if we were still young, we were already told that if we didn't behave, we would be thrown into the pits of hell. In that hot and humid place that no climate-change scenario could imagine, the sinful gay men would be surrounded by equally sinful people with horns and pointed tails, and they would all burn forever and ever to the sound of maniacal laughter from a horde functioning as the Greek chorus of a badly scripted film. And since I wanted to please my parents and harvest medals in school, I behaved.

Amen.

* * *

At the elementary school, I sat beside a boy named Roberto. He was a bit dark-skinned, with round eyes that looked like the marbles we played when we were young. And his smile, it was a megawatt smile that was enough to loosen the waistbands of your shorts and make it fall. He always copied my assignments without fail, but I let him be. He was not only gorgeous, he also shared with me his liver-spread sandwiches that their housemaid prepared for him every day that God made.

I liked eating the liver-spread sandwiches that Roberto gave me every morning. The liver spread was sweetish and brown, a bit spicy and fine-grained with what I then thought were bits of minced liver. I alternated eating it with the cheese pimiento sandwiches that our housemaid, Pilar, prepared for me every day.

Since I was only in grade I, I was demure and sweet in my dealings with Roberto. This purity in our relationship lasted all the way from grade I to grade VI. I just studied hard and learnt all of the housework. I learnt how to clean my room and wash my windows using balled-up newspaper pages, and thus cleaned the windows without leaving any trace of lint. I studied cooking under the aegis of my grandmother, who would scan the pantry and the refrigerator for whatever was at hand to cook her own version of classic Philippine cuisine from scratch. No powders, no instant something, just pure, unadulterated labour, including sitting on the small, wooden bench shaped like a lizard to shred the coconut meat against the serrated iron teeth of that small beast. My father also taught me how to press my clothes with the collar free of creases.

He said, 'My son, you should know how to cook, buy groceries from the market, do your laundry, press your clothes and clean the house . . .'

When my father would begin his lecture, I just sat and listened. Because if you just listened, it didn't mean you had to follow him, right? I listened to him because I lived for free in his house, ate the good food that he had worked hard for and he paid for the expensive tuition at the Jesuit Catholic Uni where I studied under American priests. Although my professors were Filipinos, they usually did their postgraduate studies at British or American unis, so their views were essentially white. It was the time when the foreign was in and the local was outside the academic door, paring his fingernails . . .

'I want you to learn these things not because I want you to turn into a household helper. I just want you to study overseas— as I did—that's why I want you to know all the domestic chores.

I'm teaching these lessons so you'll survive life in the real world. It's a tough world out there.'

Take note of the phrase 'as I did'. LOLs. That was my father, who studied hard at the state uni in the Philippines and landed a prestigious Fulbright Scholarship to the Wharton School of Economics. Even if I were still in grade school, my father had already mapped out his plans for me. Political science at the uni. Then the College of Law in Makati, near the Central Business District. And later, a master's in law at Harvard, no less. Yale would not be so bad. Our parents had many dreams for us, and we did our best to please them.

But I admit I wasn't as driven or as hardworking as my father. I guess I was just a good strategist. That was why I sometimes thought I would just land at Harvardian College in Cubao, Quezon City, the Philippines, and not Harvard University in Boston, Massachusetts.

That was how Roberto became my best friend in grade school. He wanted me to join the basketball team of our section because I was the tallest in class. I just told him that I had scoliosis, which I had inherited from my father. I could not afford to run around and jump, which might cause me to fall and worsen the delicate condition of my spine.

It was a fib, of course.

Because what I wanted to do was to join the volleyball team. But I had butter fingers and I seemed to be half blind. The moment I had tossed the volleyball up in the air, I could not hit it and let it fly to the enemy's side. When I hunkered down in front of the net to jump and block that volleyball, my tentacles, rather, my fingers, would get tangled in the net.

To save myself from embarrassment, I avoided all kinds of sports.

My father just enrolled me in karate. I think my father had smelt early on that his son was a Little Mermaid, who would rather hide and live under the sea even if the wicked Ursula hounded her. I did not play marbles very well, nor did I spin wooden tops as well as my male classmates did. I also never joined them in their imaginary gunfights, using wooden guns or plastic machine guns that rattled when you wound them.

Instead, I played jack stones with the little women. These were the snot-nosed girls in my neighbourhood. I always reminded them to take a bath and clear the yellow snot off their noses, otherwise, the boys would just avoid them.

I also played Chinese garter with them. Two girls would stretch a white garter between them, the height from the ground increasing after every attempt—from two feet to three feet to four feet. This was the height that I should clear with my high jump. I think a spirit would possess me when I would start my jump. I would calculate the distance between where I stood and the white garter. Then I would take a deep breath, the spirit now filling me and I would begin to run, slowly gaining speed and then I would lift off like a gazelle. Even the boys playing basketball in the nearby court would stop dead in their tracks and watch me clear the white bar, rather, the white garter. I felt as if I were flying free in the vast and open air, my wings flapping with such power and grace. For a moment, I was free from the gravity of the earth.

When my feet landed on the ground, I would look for Roberto on the basketball court. His skin would be glazed with the sweat that clung to his jersey shirt and shorts. Sometimes, I would catch him gazing at me as well. We would lock eyes for a while. I think he was amazed at how high I could jump. I was just as amazed as well, as I looked at his chest that was like a shield and then looked down at something stubborn and strong, bulging in his shiny, yellow shorts.

* * *

So, this is the real high-school life. It was so different from the sweet and saccharine song of Philippine mega-singer Sharon Cuneta. Especially if you are young, Catholic—and gay.

I thought that the whole high school, community, country, planet and universe would know that I was a Little Mermaid, but they just let it go. Maybe because I did well in school. Or I wasn't one of those 'screaming fags', as they put it. Except for once when the smelly street urchins outside the high school screamed at me and called me 'Faggot! Faggot!' as I was stepping out of the school's ornate gates. But they ran away when I went near them.

I wanted to ask them why they thought I was what they called a 'faggot'. I even wanted to offer them White Rabbit candies. Made in China and truly hard that it would break their teeth, their young yet already-rotten teeth.

I thought I was rather nice. I was already working at the *Daily Planet* newspaper when a gay, lifestyle writer told me his story. Tatiana (real name: Teodoro) always had bangs and five layers of makeup. And when he walked down the street, his hips swung from here to eternity.

He said that he was seated at the rear part of a jeepney when two young boys hitched a ride, clinging to the steel railings. They smelt of unwashed clothes, like they had been doused with a bottle of vinegar. And when they saw him, they stuck out their tongues and shouted, 'Faggot! Faggot!'

Of course, our Wonder Woman was insulted. His irritation was not helped by the humid air that seemed to enclose him in the jeep. He suddenly transformed into a dragon, and when he spoke, fire leapt from his mouth: 'Excuse me, it's okay to be gay. But what about you? Beggars!'

My jaw dropped and I told Tatiana that what he said was 'not politically correct'.

'But sir,' Tatiana replied, a glaze of wounded pride in his blue contact lenses, 'why did they have to broadcast to the whole world that I'm gay?'

'As if Batman didn't know you're gay,' piped in Joyce, the editor of the Sunday magazine, taking off her eyeglasses and looking at Tatiana down her nose.

'Not just Batman. As if Robin, who is Batman's boyfriend, doesn't know you're gay,' added Eric, who was the entertainment editor, his curly mop already alive in the early afternoon air of the newsroom.

Batman and Robin.

Hamlet and Mercutio.

Philippine national hero Dr Jose Rizal and his German best friend, Dr Ferdinand Blumentritt.

Oh my, why did I suddenly think of all these bromances?

* * *

As I was saying, I just studied hard in school until one day, Mrs Salvosa, our journalism teacher in our third year, chose me to be the associate editor of *The Laurels*. This was the school organ of our student body.

The boys even became nicer to me than they already were—especially the athletes who wanted to be featured in the school organ. In grade VI, Roberto had already flown to Canada with his family to emigrate, like a million other Filipinos leaving this godforsaken country. I was sad for a few months and waited for his letters. But even though I wrote him three letters, he never replied even once. And since I only counted up to three, I just dropped him and focused on my studies. By then, our high-school classes had already begun.

I didn't like anybody in high school, so I just let the days pass, like the yellow acacia leaves falling on the grey concrete yard of our campus. Every December, my parents brought me to watch the Holidays on Ice at the Araneta Coliseum, and we marvelled at the seemingly boneless bodies skating on such thin ice. And every May, we would go to Philippine Centre for International Trade and Exhibition, or Philcite, near Roxas Boulevard in Manila to buy my school supplies and uniform of white, polo shirt and blue trousers. I would help my three sisters with their lessons in school and every Sunday, we all went to attend the Holy Mass—even if, sometimes, I would go almost daft in the middle of the Holy Mass.

Sometimes, there would be a cute guy with a nice arse standing in front of me, distracting me from the sight of Jesus Christ hanging on the cross. I would look up at God and pray to Him: 'Please, I hope this cute guy will look at me again, so I can say to him, "Peace be with you."'

My imagination really began to fly when I reached high school. My fantasies filled me even when I was in church. Especially if the guy in front was tall, fair and cute like Leslie Cheung. Or even his partner, the unforgettable Tony Leung Chiu Wai, in the film *Happy Together*, which I saw at an art house in Manila, when I was already at university.

Oh, Blessed Virgin Mary, Mother of God, please save me from my dangerous and sinful fantasies!

* * *

Miss Azucena Inamorata Zamora, our teacher in Christian Family Life, always told us that it's a sin to be gay.

That was why we were all in the closet, hidden beneath and behind the long-sleeved shirts, the short-sleeved shirts and long trousers hanging in there. There were only a valiant few who were women in mind, heart and deed.

In a more enlightened future, they would be called the transgenders. But that would come many light years later.

In the meantime, in our high schools, we were closeted to death. Our closets felt like coffins. We could not move; we could not even breathe, lest they suspected that we were different, or very strange.

Unfortunately, or fortunately, as the case might be, Chester became my seat mate in third-year high school. May God help me, Chester's shirt always opened several buttons down on his chest. His light-brown nipples were erect and they always seemed to greet me with, 'Hello!' But I chose to ignore their greetings, since Chester with the great chest was my friend. And so, we both just concentrated on our geometry lessons, talking about hypotenuse and the perfect right angle.

My other crush was the corps commander of the Citizens' Military Training, or the CMT. His name was Valiant, because he was named after Prince Valiant with his hair cascading over his forehead like a waterfall. Valiant was tall, dark-skinned and quiet. He looked like the friend of the lead star in Philippine movies, the one who rarely had a speaking line. But when Valiant shouted his command for us every Saturday at CMT, his voice was so low and so full. He seemed to become more handsome in his military fatigue uniform.

And more than once, in my Fantasy Island at night, Prince Valiant and I would be on the beach, watching the sun go down. The sky would be streaked orange and red as Valiant and I held hands as we walked down the white beach. Then Valiant would look me in the eye, his gaze stickier than a vat of maple syrup, and kiss me till kingdom come. I would pretend to break free from his warm embrace and run away into the sunset as he chased me. And pretty soon, the darkness had fallen and my fantasy was gone.

If not Valiant, then I had fantasies with the boys in the lower sections of the high school. They were not bright, sure, but they had bodies to die for. The faces were not bad, and the muscles! There were still no gyms during those times, but there seemed to be teenagers whose bodies morphed into the letter V when they reached sixteen years of age. Muscles shaped like small buns appeared on their stomachs; their arms, thighs and legs would bulge. Indeed, these beautiful boys were proof of the existence of God.

But since Miss Azucena Inamorata Zamora of our Christian Family Life subject warned us it was a sin to be gay, we just watched but we never touched.

Touch I did only when I was already at the university. Until then, I didn't know that gays like them existed: the straight-acting ones. Because in my childhood, the only gays I saw in the movies were Dolphy and his cousin Georgie Quizon: weak and effeminate characters who were objects of fun, if not outright scorn, in those silly comedy films. Add to that the female impersonators that one saw at the fairs every fiesta: the clones of Dionne Warwick and Diana Ross and Shirley Bassey, down to the trembling eyelashes, the quivering lips and the body-hugging, mermaid gowns.

One day, we were at the fair when my father and I stopped dead in our tracks.

We saw Tina Turner in the flesh, singing 'Rolling in the River', her hair like a nest of wild and beautiful birds. Her breasts were big, her waist slim and her legs, in fishnet stockings, went on forever. Her lip-synch was pitch perfect. My jaw dropped down to my chest. But before it could drop any lower, my father had already nudged me. 'Let's move on, my son. I don't want you to end up like any of these freaks!'

Oh, I thought, Daddy-O really knew that his son wasn't only a Little Mermaid, but also a daughter of Tina Turner.

That was why I just studied hard, burning the midnight oil. I graduated valedictorian in grade school and high school. I also got a college scholarship (for tuition and fees plus stipend and book allowance; may you all die of envy). My father was delighted, because he would save more than one million pesos for my university education. He could then use the money to send my siblings to school.

And I was surprised to see so many good-looking men at the university. There were fair-skinned mestizos of Spanish and Filipino blood. Chinese Filipinos. Indian Filipinos. Foreigners from the USA, Canada and Ireland. And the seemingly pure Filipinos: tall and dark and handsome, dark as the most delicious chocolate.

* * *

I first met Angus at the university. Oy, it's not Angus beef, but a friend of mine from England.

Angus was the son of the British ambassador, and we became classmates at the university. Angus was taller than I was, had freckles on his face and his eyes changed colour from blue to green, depending on the slant of the light. One day, we were eating at the cafeteria in the residence halls where we could see the mountains of Antipolo under a vast, white, cloudless sky.

I said, 'You know, Angus, your eyes have the same colour as the mountains in the distance.'

'Oh really, Jon?' he said in that crisp English with an upper-crust accent. The mere mention of the letter 'o' in 'Jon' already wanted me to say 'yes' to him.

'Indeed,' I said instead. 'Their colour alternates between blue and green, depending on the sunlight.' I was trying to wax poetic because I desperately wanted him to like me.

He smiled and then I saw his very white teeth again. The brilliance of the teeth of all the models of Close-Up toothpaste were nothing compared to the whiteness of his teeth.

'We only just arrived in Manila last month. Would you like to come to my house this weekend? I will cook something English for you.'

Why not? I wanted to say. But instead, I tried to be very proper and said instead, 'If it will not be too much of an inconvenience for you . . .'

'Oh, no, I would be delighted if you could visit me this weekend.'

'Yes, of course,' I answered, then I placed some sisig on my plate. 'Angus, do you want some, ahhhh, sliced ears and cheeks of a pig? They've been grilled rather nicely.'

He looked at the dish, then he just smiled at me, because he was a diplomat's son. But his smile was tight, like a straight line, and it didn't show any of his teeth. That, and the look he gave me seemed to tell me that EEEWWWW was what he really wanted to say.

Angus and his family rented a mansion at Forbes Park, an exclusive enclave for the wealthy in the central business district of Makati. My father drove me to my visit to the house of Angus, and he was so glad I had a friend who lived there.

'That's right, son,' he said, while steering his trusted blue Toyota Corolla. 'Cultivate your contacts, your social networks. The leaders of tomorrow will come from your university. Be friends with all of them, especially the rich and the well-connected.'

This was the way my father spoke. Always looking for the best opportunities even if he were just driving a simple car. On the way to the mansion where Angus lived, we met Mitsubishi Pajeros and breezy BMWs, even a Jaguar or two, but our humble Toyota Corolla ignored all of them. We finally found the mansion in a cul-de-sac. It was as big as all the other houses that preened like self-important matrons in Forbes Park.

I kissed the hand of my father before I left his car. I also told him I would just grab a cab to go home so there was no need for him to pick me up later. He gave me a crisp bill of 500 pesos. Oh, so nice, I thought.

'Oh, this is for you. I gave you extra money. I know that you too have a monthly stipend from your scholarship, but it's always good to have some extra funds. For sundry expenses.'

That was the way my father spoke. A bit strange, his English seeming to come from the last century.

I waved at my father and pretty soon, our Toyota Corolla was gone.

I pressed the button on the concrete post beside the tall, brown gate. A housemaid with a face lightened by papaya soap and wearing a starched, white uniform opened the gate and asked, 'Are you Diyan, the classmate of Sir Angus?'

I nodded and Inday ushered me into the yard.

A big fountain bloomed in the middle of the garden. A young, male angel made of stone was holding a trumpet, and from this trumpet gushed clear water. The garden was well trimmed and colour-coordinated. Green plants with long leaves were planted near the wall, while in front stood smaller plants with leaves of various colours: yellow, red, violet and white. A koi pond curved near the grand mahogany door. The fish—mostly orange, dotted with white and black—looked fat and well fed, unlike the emaciated fish in the ill-maintained Manila Zoo, where the poorly fed fish glided in a languid fashion.

'Hey, Jon, over here!' said Angus. He was wearing a white T-shirt and blue shorts. Colour-coordinated as well, with the housemaid. I wanted to tease him, but I just bit my tongue because he might not feed me. I was already hungry.

Angus led the way into his house. Curves of leaves and curlicues of grapes were carved on the thick, mahogany door. Angus opened the door and ushered me in. A blast of the air-conditioner greeted me. Indeed, I am now in cold and clean England. My arse seemed to sink as I sat down on the olive-coloured sofa. I noticed that rich people didn't like stark colours. Not green but olive. Not blue but aquamarine. The big, wooden coffee table seemed to have come from one of the tribes in Mindanao in the southern Philippines, deep dark wood, flecked with mother-of-pearl shells that had been cut and shaped into diamonds.

'You just sit here while I prepare your food. I've made something special for you. Hamburger with mashed potato.'

I just blinked in disbelief that I had come all the way here for a Jollibee hamburger.

'But worry not. I also prepared a rhubarb, gingernut cheesecake for you. Veddy English!'

'Thank you.' It was my turn to give him a tight smile. 'Sounds delicious—and very special, indeed.' But the thought that dear, cute Angus would cook my pedestrian hamburger made me widen my smile.

Angus was standing under the grand chandelier in their living room, the wash of yellow light flowing down to where we sat. And in that spot, the colours of Angus's eyes changed. Sometimes blue, sometimes green. Like the sea water in Palawan.

The hamburger was soft and the rhubarb was, ahhhh, strange. Its sweetness was overpowered by the ginger. And when he invited me to watch the telly in his room, who was I to say no? I followed Angus (nice arse, a football player, his legs and thighs dusted with fine gold hairs) into his room. I softly closed the door behind me.

* * *

I had thought that Angus was a rice queen, those White guys who liked brown Barbies like me. I thought that he would do something delightful to me in his big and cool room.

But indeed, we just watched the telly in his room. We watched football on ESPN. 'There goes my favourite team, the Manchester United! Do you also have football teams in the Philippines?'

We had *sipa*, or *sepak takraw*, I wanted to tell him in a slightly piqued manner, which used a synthetic plastic, or rattan, ball instead of a regular football. I was pissed because I had thought we would watch gay porn from Bel Ami and then he would do to me what we saw on the telly. But instead, we watched Manchester United! But of course, I still had to be diplomatic.

'Oh, I'm afraid we don't have them at the moment. But you never know when some British-Filipino player will emerge from nowhere and jumpstart an interest in football here in the Philippines.'

And so, we watched football, as my eyes took in the details of Angus's room. A square mirror framed in deeply stained wood, a wardrobe the colour of old wine, a big armchair upholstered in soft, grey velvet. Oh, these rich people. As I had said earlier, they didn't like stark and strong colours. Not black but grey. Always restrained. Always controlled. Like gays in the closet.

And of course, I also stole sidelong glances at Angus's legs. We sat beside each other on the sofa upholstered in what looked like blue denim. Very hip, indeed. The golden hair on his legs and thighs looked so fine. I curbed the impulse to touch them. I just kicked the impulse away, the way the players on the screen kicked the football until it flew like a bird in the air.

After watching the telly, Angus gave me a tour of his house and showed me the kidney-shaped swimming pool, lustrous with water under a tropical sky; and later, it was time to say goodbye. He had asked their driver to bring me home in their Ford Escalade.

I took a shower upon reaching home, then turned on the telly and watched the old *Charlie's Angels*. I liked the blond curls of Farrah Fawcett and I really identified with her: brave and slim, her smile like a brilliant ray of sunlight.

* * *

One day, Angus invited me out to have drinks at an English pub in Makati. He really liked to drink, but he was often in the company of his friends from the same rich neighbourhoods, or his high-school classmates at the International School in Manila. It was the kind of group where you would hear five different English accents around one table.

It was the Christmas holidays and Angus didn't join his parents for their annual leave to go home to England. We were about to graduate from the university and Angus said he was behind with the research for his thesis. It's because you're like a tortoise, I had wanted to tease him. And you also kept on changing your topic for the thesis. So, while most of us were already done with our research, Angus was still groping around for his research questions, before he could do the annotated bibliography and quickly dash the first draft of his paper.

We went to Greenbelt and entered a pub. The place was jumping! People from various countries filled the pub, their faces now turning red with the liquors being imbibed. The walls were made of real oak. Wooden barrels of beer were set up on the bar, with high stools covered in cool black leather. Hundreds of bottles of different wines and liquors were lined up in front of me. As the hours ticked by, the expats slowly vanished one by one; yet Angus and I kept on drinking.

He ordered Guinness beer, which had a malty sweetness and a hoppy bitterness to it. I didn't like it too much. I ordered San Miguel beer instead for my second round. I stopped on the third round because I didn't want to feel bloated. I just kept on eating the fish and chips that Angus had ordered. The breading was fried to a crisp, but the haddock fish was soft. It was served with malt vinegar and lemon, and with tartar sauce for the dip. I loved it!

I just kept talking and listening to Angus that night. He seemed to be a different person, though. He was more talkative and his voice seemed to rise a pitch higher. So, this was what he looked like when drunk. He rarely partook of the *calamares* he had ordered, and the delicious, deep-fried squid rings lay untouched on the table. 'Your country has the best seafood in the world,' he said. Or rather, slurred. Then he kept on ordering and drinking Guinness beer, truly dark and truly potent. He seemed to be drowning something inside him.

And of course, I was concerned. Why would the rest of the world not call us 'hospitable' if I could not express concern for a cute foreigner getting wasted before my very eyes?

'Are you all right, Angus?' I asked.

'Not really,' he slurred.

'Oh, what happened? Are you still sad about your late thesis? I can help you with that since I'm almost done with mine.'

He just looked at me for a while. His eyes were glazed, either from the vast amounts of alcohol he had already imbibed, or by something else that lay deep inside him. I wasn't sure whether he would smile or cry. Then his true confession began.

'My partner and I, we just broke up. That's the real reason I didn't join my parents for our Christmas holidays back in London. I didn't want to see Mark there.'

'Mark?' I said aloud. And in my thoughts the words swam: Not Marsha? Marcia? Marimar? Marbella?

'Yes, Mark,' he said, a bitter smile dawning on him after he saw my crestfallen face. 'Why? Didn't you know that I'm gay?'

I thought that my eyes must've grown as big as my whole face. 'No, you don't have any trace . . .'

'Oh, stop it, Jon,' he said. 'Only in your country. Of course, you also have straight-acting gays here. Only they're deep in the closet, full of fears. I should know. I used to be in the deepest part of the closet myself . . .'

Oh, so Angus became my friend because he had sensed my gayness. And it was also clear to me that he only wanted to be friends with me. A confidante. Like a soul sister? But I still liked Angus, even though I knew he too was gay like me. I wanted to comfort him, to place my arms around him and tell him everything would be all right, and that I would always be there for him . . .

* * *

One day, I decided to make an anonymous confession to Papa Jack, a famous disc jockey in the AM radio band.

Yes, Papa Jack, all the green and dirty plans in my mind that night didn't happen. Angus's driver picked us up in the Ford Escalade and first brought him home because he was already truly wasted. Then, I was driven back to my house in Quezon City. Angus returned to England after his studies at the university, and oh yes, he did finish his thesis in time. I just helped him in the final stretches of his research and writing.

Yes, Papa Jack, I was sad at first, but you know gays like me, we rebound very quickly. Like the famous basketball players of my country, we are always quick and good in the hardcourt.

So, I went to the library. Yes, I went to the library of our university and read the few books there on homosexuality. I also went to the British Council Library at its old address in New Manila, a white mansion with a tower at the back. It also had a garden filled with marigolds and roses. I also borrowed books from the Thomas Jefferson Library at its old address in Makati, a grey building whose air-conditioner was so chilly it seemed to remind you of New York City in a deep freeze.

I borrowed gay books. I read novels, short stories and essays that dealt with the so-called 'gay experience'. I was like a teacher in methods of research who had gone berserk. A teacher who did research to heal his heartbreak.

My main influence then was *A Boy's Own Story*, the autobiographical novel by Edmund White, about a fifteen-year-old boy's awakening to his gayness. I finished reading it in a day, my heart in my throat. I read a lot and thought a lot so that I would be more prepared if I come out (as I had not yet come out at that time). But you know how closet cases are—they're the last to know that they are gay. Everyone knows that you're a Super Girl or a Super Woman or a Ford Model, but you would not admit it to yourself.

Oh, I'm sorry, Papa Jack. Let us get back to my story. Life has so many distractions. How did my family discover my secret? Like a typical Filipino family, we did not talk much about it. But ever since I was young, I was already being compared to my male cousins.

They would say, 'Oy, your cousin likes basketball. Why don't you like it too?'

I wanted to counter, 'Well, he might be good at basketball, but he always sat in row four, the last row in school, because he's an idiot.'

Or: 'Oy, your cousin is good at boxing, how about you?'

I wanted to counter, 'Well, he might be good at boxing, but he also looks like the ugly boxer, Manny Pacquiao, who considered gays "worse than animals".' So never mind. Later, after that boxer issued his virulent and homophobic remark, I posted in my Facebook: 'At last, we have now discovered the missing link between the Cro-Magnon and humans.' An eye for an eye and a tooth for a tooth, then.

But in reality, I liked sports, too. As far back as grade school, I was already in the track-and-field team. Before the start of the athletic competition, I would hear people say, 'Oy, too bad. That one is a faggot.'

Really? Let us see.

After the 100-metre dash was over, who won? It was the faggot who won. It was like this, Papa Jack.

I always joined the 100-metre dash. I would fly, errr, run like a gazelle. I would feel as if I was running with my long hair braided into two pigtails. And then the boys would be running after me. So, there I was, tall and beautiful and swift, with the boys chasing me. *Andale, andale,* Speedy Gonzales, *arriva, arriva, andale.* So, like the quick mouse of our afternoon cartoon shows, I flew straight into the finish line. Gold medals. Always. And a mark of 100 in my physical education class.

That was the way I always served revenge on those who called me a faggot in the athletic competitions. Revenge was always served cold. With gold medals.

I always watched whenever Muhammad Ali had a boxing match. As Ali, who had the charm of the devil, said, 'Float like a butterfly, sting like a bee.' I was there at the Araneta Coliseum with my father when Joe Frazier and Muhammad Ali fought at the 'Thrilla in Manila'. My father brought me there, to watch the modern gladiators clash in the biggest coliseum in the 20th century.

I also watched basketball games on the telly. But I was just pissed when the shorts of the basketball players got longer and longer. Their shorts used to be very abbreviated; you could always see the shape of Felix the cat.

I also liked aikido. I could break the elbow of anyone who would try to harm me, especially those who waited in dark corners at night while I waited for a cab to bring me home. One-two-three in a quick, fluid and graceful motion, then snap!

You were asking me, Papa Jack, if my parents knew about my gayness?

Well, I think they did. Because, when I was young, my father always told me to carry my books sideways. 'Do not,' he would often remind me, 'do not hold your books across your chest!' I had wanted to retort to Father Dearest that I was covering my boobs with my books because the naughty boys in school wanted to take a peek at them. But, of course, I did not say so because I did not want Father Dearest to thrash me with his leather belt.

The gays during my time were also impersonators in fiestas, as I have already said, or objects of fun in films, or hairdressers! Yes, like Benny, the Hairdresser, with his fake eyelashes, which were curly and one-mile long.

Because the gays were closeted during those times, they were sad and vinegary. Their noses were always scrunched up in dismay, as if they had just smelt chicken shit. And I didn't want to end up like them, Papa Jack. I didn't want to be like bitter gourd.

Don't you agree, Papa Jack, that we should all just be happy and gay?

* * *

Papa Jack gave such wise advice that I decided to send him a second anonymous confession a week later.

Because you told me that my first anonymous confession to you was a smash, this is part two of my confession, done upon your behest.

So, what I did, Papa Jack, was that I studied hard. This was also my counsel to gay students like myself. Study hard. Or to gays who were already working. Work hard. Damn the torpedoes, as those cute seamen, I mean, seafarers, would put it in the old Hollywood movies.

I read gay books. I joined gay organizations because they are also support groups. And if there was a cute, gay man who was my crush and who also liked me, then we would just hook up with each other and have sex until the end of the world. Ooops! Papa Jack, that was just a joke. Please don't turn off my microphone. You knew very well that your radio station is the only one we listen to. The only one we could trust. Those of us who were broken-hearted and lost in the darkness. Those of us caught in the love's spider web.

And how did my family come to know? Wasn't that your last question, Papa Jack?

Everything started with a T-shirt. Yes, Papa Jack, with a T-shirt. I had a Filipino-American friend named Zach. He also liked rainbows and he was a friend of Dorothy as well; *The Wizard of Oz* was his favourite film. In short, Papa Jack, he was gay like me. If one day he and I were to die, we would just slide up and down the rainbow, singing our deathless anthem, 'Somewhere'.

Anyway, highway, by the way, Zach gave me a wonderful white T-shirt. And what did the T-shirt say? An image of two straight-looking guys was imprinted down the middle of the T-shirt. They were stark naked. They were kissing and hugging. And beneath them was emblazoned the words, 'Safe sex is the best sex.' That was all.

Were you asking me what the problem was, Papa Jack? It seemed like a harmless enough T-shirt promoting safe sex, but this was what happened. I always brought my laundry to my parents' house every weekend so that the laundry woman could wash, dry and iron them. I didn't know that this T-shirt was included in my other clothes that I had brought home that weekend. So, our laundry woman was soaking the T-shirt in the suds of white Perla soap when she raised it and screamed, EEEEEEK! That was the scream that came from her, a scream that a whole block in the neighbourhood heard loud and clear. My grandmother came running. This was my formidable grandmother from the Bicol Region, whom everybody feared, and whose favourite cuss word was 'your mother's cunt!'

'Whose T-shirt is that?' she demanded, ready to breathe fire and singe the skin of the laundry woman. Even if my grandmother had a rather filthy mouth, she always attended Sunday Mass with a white veil on her head and a holy brown scapular like a protective talisman around her neck.

When the laundry woman mentioned my name, my grandmother wanted to slap her with the bar of white Perla laundry soap. 'That's not true!' she snapped. 'That T-shirt cannot be his!'

Oh, I did love my grandmother because she was the one who used to take care of me while my parents were away at work. She would put Vicks VapourRub on my temples, my neck, back, and my chest when I had cold. She also brought me with her to

Manila, to visit her seamstress daughter in Old Santa Mesa, during Christmas and she even bought me a toy gun. Yes, indeed. A toy gun bought in Quiapo that went rat-tat-tat-tat and was the envy of my straight cousins. I wanted to tell my cousins they could have this stupid gun and give me Barbie any time, but I did not give voice to my thoughts. I was afraid of my grandmother's tongue, and her fingers that would pinch our groin or wring our ears whenever we did not wake up early to go to school, or whenever we did not help the housemaid with the chores at home and in the garden.

Sometimes, she would even ask me about my girlfriend, and I would always reply, 'But Grandma, I'm too busy in school to think of girls. Didn't you say we should focus on our studies and become a lawyer, or a doctor, or an engineer, or an architect, or work overseas and make a lot of money?' Whenever I lied to her, I could feel my nose becoming longer and longer, like Pinocchio's. Even when she was already on her death bed and hallucinating that my long-dead grandfather was waiting at the foot of her bed to fetch her, she was still asking me, 'When will you get married to a woman?'

I had wanted to tell her that I was not a lesbian. But had I confessed to her that, yes, one day, I would marry, but I would marry another man, she would have died right then and there. Her soul, may the Lord bless it, would be quickly transported in front of Saint Peter, who would weigh her filthy words vis-à-vis her Sunday rituals of piety. So, when she was already gasping for her last breath and still asking me when would I marry a woman, I just bit my lower lip and did not answer her query.

Then my father also arrived on the scene. The laundry woman, God did not bless her, also showed the controversial T-shirt to my father and told him that it belonged to me.

Silence. The silence of the lambs. A silence so thick you could collect it and put it in the fridge, then cut it up and use it as lard to cook the fried garlic rice for breakfast the next morning.

But trust my businessman father to collect his wits as quickly as possible. He just said, 'Well, maybe my son is now into niche marketing.' I think it must have dawned upon him that his son, indeed, is a denizen of Dorothy. And what could he do, except make the best of a 'bad' situation, as was his wont?

And that, Papa Jack, was how I came out to my family. That was why I believe in the utter power and innate magic of T-shirts. Do you also want to have a gay T-shirt, Papa Jack?

* * *

Because I read a lot of books and studied hard at university, I received a general weighted average of 3.85. I applied for scholarships to graduate schools in the United States and was lucky to get one for a master's in English at Rutgers University, the State University of New Jersey.

* * *

'Paging Juan de la Cruz, paging Juan de la Cruz, your passport is with the security office.'

When I heard my name and the word 'passport', my skin crawled. I realized in a flash what had happened: I had taken my passport from my passport holder, slung on a string around my neck, put it in a transparent plastic envelope and had joined the queue. It was a long queue of passengers who had just arrived at the John F. Kennedy Airport in New York City. It was the first of August and I had just arrived after a direct flight from Manila to New York City aboard United Airlines.

I went to the security office and said my name. The woman holding my passport looked like Angela Lansbury, down to the eyeglasses attached to a string. She looked at the photograph in the passport, then touched the sides of her eyeglasses and brought them down by a fraction of an inch and looked at me.

'Oh, this is you all right. Next time, sonny, be careful with your passport.' She smiled kindly and I smiled back, collected my passport and returned to my queue.

People from the developing world who were coming to the United States for the first time have steeled themselves for this. I presented my passport to the thirty-something-year-old man along with the sealed, white envelope that contained my papers as the holder of an F-1 student visa. The American embassy in Manila processed my visa and the consul told me to present the unopened envelope to the immigration officer at the airport in the USA.

The man had hazel eyes and he ripped open the side of the envelope quickly. He seemed to have torn so many envelopes in his life that he did it in seconds, extracted the sheaf of papers from within and glanced at it. He seemed to be the type of person who could read a page by letting his eyes follow the shape of the letter Z.

His eyes zipped down my paper, then he stamped my passport and returned it to me. 'Good luck with your studies,' he said without smiling, 'and welcome to the United States of America.'

It was only August, but a chill ran down my spine the moment the doors of the airport opened. It was cold. I quickly put on the grey, winter coat which my father had bought for me, and I towed my big, blue suitcase, filled with 50 kilograms of things from home. Earlier, or more precisely, twenty-four hours ago, I had been in Manila.

My mother was the one who packed my suitcase. She had never travelled overseas but she knew that shirts and trousers had to be rolled, socks turned into balls and all documents had to be sorted and stored in a transparent plastic envelope for easy retrieval.

I let her do my packing, if that made her happy. I would just bite my tongue and quell the urge to say, 'It is my luggage, Mama, let me pack it.'

By instinct she knew what to put in there: my favourite pyjamas, shorts and shirts, as well as the new wardrobe that I had bought in the last month before I left Manila. I had scoured the surplus shops and bought several long-sleeved, turtle-necked shirts, windbreakers and jackets. My father gave me the winter coat, which he had bought on a stopover in Dubai on his way home to the Philippines.

My father drove our blue Toyota and my mother sat beside him, while I sat at the back. We did not bring our grandmother because she had not stopped weeping. My fierce grandmother had lost weight and had become an emotional one. She cried her eyes out when she saw me with the suitcase and my clothes—a blue, turtle-necked shirt that sheathed my thin body.

'You'll be gone for a long time and when you come back, I shall already be dead,' she wailed.

I just went to her and kissed her on the cheeks, my grandmother who had taken care of me. Since my father simultaneously worked and then took his BA and later his law studies, and my mother taught music even on weekends, it was my grandmother who brought me up. My father had told me stories about my grandmother smoking her black Bataan cigarette with the lighted end inside her mouth while doing the laundry that consisted of napkins filled with my baby shit.

'But your grandmother ignored your shit and just scrubbed the fabric with soap and squeezed and scrubbed and squeezed,' said my father. His stories could leap higher than the roosters that he raised and sometimes brought to the cockfights held at the end of the month outside the military airbase.

Now, I saw the blue van that would take us to the Regent Hotel, after which I would take the Princeton van that would drop me off at Rutgers University. The blue van was immediately filled with what looked like several undergraduate students wearing just shirts and shorts in that cold day of early spring. I deposited my suitcase at the back of the van and sat by the window. I immediately fished out my mobile phone and sent a text message to my friend, Leo.

'Here in the van bound for the uni. 2 p.m. New York City time.'

I pressed send and, in a few seconds, I got a reply. It was already 2 a.m. in Manila but Leo was still awake.

'Any cuties in the van?'

'Undergraduate students going to Rutgers and Princeton. I am the oldest of them at twenty-five.'

'Are there any boys?'

'Yes. Three. Blond hair and blue eyes and legs that stretch for 1,000 miles.'

Leo sent three big smile emojis, I sent one smile and then, I turned off my phone. The student beside me was looking at my phone and wondering what I was doing. There were still no text messages in American mobile phones in August of 2000, but it was already popular in the Philippines. Well, our landline telephones hardly worked anyway, which was why mobile phones were our preferred medium of communication.

We reached the New Jersey Turnpike, a long freeway that looked like a grey razor blade. Some big factories slouched beside the highway, but they looked old and abandoned. The undergraduates were soon asleep, and I took a nap as well. We were awakened by the voice of our driver, who said we had reached Regent Hotel and should wait for the Princeton shuttle van.

I got off the shuttle van, heaved my suitcase down and walked into the hotel lobby. I went to the toilet and asked the young doorman to please keep an eye on my suitcase. 'It came from so far away,' I said, and he smiled as well.

More old factories awaited us as we navigated our way from the hotel to New Brunswick, where Rutgers University was located. The Princeton shuttle van deposited me on George Street, in front of a big, red-brick building. It looked exactly like what I saw in the photograph: Dear Murray Hall, where the department of English was housed.

Rutgers University was located in New Brunswick, a commuter town. You needed to take the free shuttle-buses to transfer from one building to another in the vast university. It was that big, as big as the town of Los Baños in Laguna, where a satellite campus of the University of the Philippines sprawled serenely, near the hump-backed mountains.

I quickly joined GaySoc, or the gay society. We had discussion sessions on homosexuality and visited the gay bars of New York City as a group. New York was only an hour away from my university.

It must have been the colour of my skin, or the fact that I looked much younger than my twenty-five years, or my facility with the English language, or just the plain, discreet charm of the bourgeoisie (I wish), but the young and cute White boys always talked to me. I just fenced words with them. I had mastered the American art of the banter: a quick smile here, a witty word there, and laughter with your head raised, your long, slim neck shaped like a vase.

On rare occasions, I would go home with one of them, to his home, to play Scrabble with him. Joke. Or we would play Snakes and Ladders. But more of Snakes and Ladders than Scrabble— but the games only involved Snakes!

However, after several months, I grew tired of this kind of lifestyle. And the only thing, as Oscar Wilde said, that we should avoid is boredom. You sleep with someone who catches your fancy in a bar, come with him to his house and then in the morning, you wake up beside this complete stranger. And that was how I met Steve. He was working at the university. He was younger than me, at twenty. He had blond hair and blue eyes, and he was hard working, a typical New Jersey guy. He was also bright and good-looking, but always possessed with a sense of sadness.

He became my boyfriend in the United States. We were together for almost two years when I was taking my master's programme there. He even asked me to live with him. I moved into his apartment in New Brunswick three months into our relationship, but I insisted on paying my share of the rent. I cooked chicken *adobo* for him, the slices of chicken fragrant in their stew of soy sauce, vinegar, laurel leaves and brown sugar. I also cooked his other favourite, beef *caldereta*, the slices of beef soft and melting in their stew of tomato sauce with potatoes, carrots and again, brown sugar.

For his part, he could only boil potatoes for me, and I always teased him about it. His repartee would be, 'That's okay, because you taste better than your chicken adobo.' You would be crazy to believe everything that your partner told you, nevertheless it sent a thrill running down my spine.

The two years just flew on the swiftest of wings. I had to return to the Philippines after my Master of Arts programme of study. I could not continue with my PhD studies because I had to return and stay in the Philippines for two years, as part of the requirements for my scholarship. Our farewell was like a scene from a film. He drove me in his old car to the John F. Kennedy Airport in New York City. My flight was at eight o' clock in the evening, with stopovers in Detroit and Narita International Airport in Tokyo.

Upon reaching the parking lot at the JFK Airport, he wordlessly turned to me and kissed me. He was crying as he embraced me tightly, as if never wanting to let me go. I was also sad, but I didn't weep. My grandfather, bless that crazy old soldier, taught me to be stoic. All my life, even in the face of life's gravest conditions, I never showed any emotion. A thick mask shielded me from my deepest feelings.

'I love you too,' I told him. I kissed him, brushing my lips lightly against his lips, and then, I turned my back and opened the door. The sun was beginning to go down, and the sky of New York was streaked with orange and red. The air seemed to be holding its breath. I extracted my suitcase from the boot of his car and then I walked away without looking back at him.

My heart was like a piece of paper, shredded to bits.

* * *

For a year, Steve and I wrote letters to each other. I sent him airmail letters written on thin, blue aerogramme paper with prepaid stamps. He sent me letters in his chicken scrawl handwriting on thick paper. Sometimes we would call each other on the telephone. There was no international direct-dialling at that time, or even a fax system. We would route our calls through a telephone operator, and the bills were sky high. And then he stopped writing. Just like that. He merely said, 'I can no longer bear the pain of this long-distance relationship. There's no certainty that you will come back to me,' his last letter had said. 'And anyway, I no longer receive any letter from you—" Which was a lie, since I was writing to him on a regular basis. In fact, I had already bought many years' supply of the blue aerogramme, because I was ready for the long haul.

But he just vanished, like a spiral of grey smoke into the air. My days were flat and they had no taste. I survived them through the sheer shield of my stoicism. I just focused on my work, avoided watching love stories in the cinema and turned off the radio when a love song went on air. In my mind, I had dug a hole and buried Steve there. That, I thought, would be the best way to survive when you no longer have a heart, but just a gaping hole in your chest.

I was able to return to the United States only after three years. I had to save up to be able to make a short visit there, to check out universities that had offered me scholarships for my PhD. I arrived at the beginning of spring. A bracing coldness filled the air. The flowers were just unfurling their petals to the sun, and the maple trees were sprouting fresh leaves.

I took the New Jersey Express train from 32nd Street in New York to New Brunswick. I intended to collect some of my clothes and the books which I had left with Steve.

He still lived in the same apartment, in a leafy cul-de-sac filled with birch trees. He opened the white door; his smile was wan. He embraced me tearfully. Sparta was back in his stoic mood. But I felt not just stoic but pissed as well.

He was blubbering about not having received any more of my letters that was why he had stopped writing. 'Well, I'm only here to pick up the clothes and books which I had left with you. I need those books for my PhD studies here,' I replied, sitting down on the sofa with its worn upholstery of faded blue.

He sat down beside me and suddenly, in an awkward movement, he tried to kiss me on the lips. EEEEWWWW. So that was how it felt, when all the love you had for someone had already melted. Like butter out in the sun. I turned my face away. One day, I just woke up and discovered that I no longer loved Steve. And because of the 10,000 miles and the lack of attention, I was swamped by sadness and later found out that all of my feelings were gone. Like the morsels of food swallowed up and churned into bits by those efficient contraptions in modern American kitchens.

He told me I could get my things together while he went out to the supermarket to rustle up some things to cook for me. I went into the bedroom that I had shared with him for a year. It was still the same—dirty clothes on the floor like the flaked-off skin of some prehistoric beast. I even found packets of condoms on his side table—as if he wanted to slap me with the information that he was now having sex with someone new. Well, he could even swallow the whole of New Jersey and I couldn't care less.

I would not even care if his dick had shrunk down to the size of a needle and disappeared into thin air!

I was looking for my clothes and books in his closet when the letters just tumbled over, one by one. My letters in their thin blue aerogrammes! They drifted down to the floor like broken wings.

He arrived with the groceries in brown shopping bags. He hadn't even put down the bags on the dining table, when I showed him my letters, now scattered on the floor.

He turned paler than his usual, White-American paleness. The blueness of his eyes turned so dark blue that they were almost black. He burst into tears.

'I couldn't bear it any more. The fact that you left me. Every day. I would stare at the packets of Mama Sita tamarind broth that you left in my pantry. I would talk to the packets as if that were you, asking you to come back.'

Idiot! I wanted to holler at him. That damned packet would not answer you, of course, because it was just meant to sour the broth for a dish of vegetables and pork!

But I just looked at him coldly, in my mask of Sparta: stoic, solid and sure.

'Every morning, I would stare at the green rubber shoes that you left by the door. Its toes were pointed towards me, as if telling me you would come back. But you were gone, and God knows how terrible that feeling was. The days and nights of your absence!'

Aye, these White men, I wanted to tell him. So spineless and so weak. Acting as if they were Blanche Du Bois in Tennessee Williams's play, *A Streetcar Named Desire*. It's because they didn't have to contend with those horrible tropical storms that would drag the dead bodies miles away from where they used to live. Or a volcanic eruption that wiped out one's house and one's childhood village. Or a military dictatorship without end, where the children of the dictator just took over his mantle and continued to pillage the country the way their mad father and his extravagant wife did.

Just a few years' absence and he already felt like this, as limp as a rag?

He clung to me, crying his eyes out over my shoulder. I just let him be. I didn't return his embrace or even attempt to console him.

He continued, 'Now, I see your suitcase. You're leaving me again! I still love you. So much.'

But what could I do? I wanted to ask him. I wanted to tell him that I had been offered several scholarships for my PhD programme. One of the offers came from New York University, which was only an hour's train ride away from New Jersey. But what would be the point of telling him that?

I had moved on. So sorry. When you stopped writing to me, I picked up the fragments of myself scattered all over the floor and put them back together all over again. Slowly and painstakingly. And decided that whatever I would do with my life I would do solely for my sake, not for someone else. Especially not for a non-performing ex-boyfriend in deepest, darkest New Jersey.

Later, while I was hauling my blue suitcase on my way to the train station, beside the bushes alive with daisies and magnolias, I told myself I still cared for him. Sure. But it is now different. An old photograph which had faded, and his face had been blurred.

Let me paraphrase a French writer whose words I had read in a novel: There are many rooms in our hearts. And the people we love live inside these rooms. Sometimes, we would end up locking one of the rooms. At other times, we just keep the door open. In the end, only you will decide which door will remain open or closed.

And which door would be shut forever and ever with a loud, resounding thud. PAK!

GHOSTS

All my life I have kept company with ghosts. That is why I do not like watching horror movies. Invariably, the dead people are portrayed with blood-streaked faces and twisted limbs and having a very bad hair day. Or they are depicted dragging chains on full moon nights and making heavy wooden doors creak and groan.

But that is not how I have seen or heard the dead at all. When I was seven years old, my maternal grandmother died. I knew her slightly, but whenever I visited Oas, Albay, my parents' hometown, she would ask me the usual questions: 'Did you like the food? How is school? Does your mother teach you to play the piano?' She used to be fat, her high soprano reverberating around the church during Sunday Mass. When she became older, she looked diminished; thinner, her hair cascading down her bony shoulders like a thin waterfall.

One day, a telegram informed us that she had died of tuberculosis. My mother went to her room and wept quietly. Later, she packed her clothes, along with my father's clothes and my sisters'. I didn't go with them because my final examinations were approaching.

I was left in the care of my paternal grandmother and the housemaids. Lola Juana was footloose and would take me everywhere with her. I read her *Aliwan Komiks* and *Liwayway* magazine every week and listened to the nightly radio programmes with her. When I had a fever, she would cook chicken congee for me and prepare a warm drink of ginger tea with a dash of small lemons. On the night that my parents and sisters went home to Albay, I slept beside her in her room which she always locked in the night.

However, the next morning, I was found asleep on the floor of the living room.

The housemaids were frightened. They told me that my dead grandmother must have taken me by the hand and led me to sleep outside because I had not gone home to attend her funeral. Lola Juana remained silent in her room, praying quietly for the soul of my other grandmother. Both old women had been neighbours and good friends. And then my lola assured me that everything would be all right. When my parents and sisters returned, it was a long time before I could look at the photographs of my dead grandmother. She was wearing her blue Catholic Women's League uniform. Small balls of cotton plugged her nose, her eyes seemingly weighed down by stones.

A year later, we were having breakfast on a cool morning. The previous night had been stormy. Rain had lashed the java plum trees outside and the wind had keened in the dark. The radio was turned to the news (a grisly murder, a corrupt politician; some things never change). Then suddenly, somebody knocked on the door.

My father answered it. He came back, crestfallen. 'A C-47 plane has just crashed in Lubao.' I knew that some of the passengers in the plane were my parents' friends. My father changed into his fatigue uniform and rushed out. I ran to him.

He asked, 'Do you want to join me?'

I said, 'Yes,' and off we went.

In the early morning, the wind was like a chilly breath against my skin. When we reached the hospital, the first ambulance was just arriving. The siren wailed. The red light flashing on its roof looked like a wounded eye. The hospital attendants in green cotton uniforms ran down the stairs. The ambulance doors flew open. On the stretcher lay a man, his fatigue uniform torn around the elbows and knees. His leather boots were gone. I remember him as my father's friend who was a good chess player, plotting the moves of the wooden chess pieces in his mind. But now, his eyes were closed. Another stretcher bore a woman. Her blue dress was drenched with blood. I remember her as my mother's fellow teacher in the elementary school, the one who always brought vases of beautiful roses in front of the altar of the Blessed Virgin Mary in the military chapel when the flowers she had tended at home bloomed in profusion. I felt something rising in my throat. A sudden warmth spread through my nose. Everything felt fuzzy. Then another ambulance came, its wail shattering the morning air into so many fragments. I saw my vomit darken the earth, through a film of my own tears.

During the wake, I refused to enter the chapel at first. Later, with one of our housemaids, I went into the chapel and sat at the back. Forty-one coffins crowded the chapel. My friend's father, a military captain who used to arrange my friend's cub-scout neck-kerchief, died. His sixteen-year-old daughter had also died. Her boyfriend, all of eighteen years old, just stood in front of her coffin during the days of the wake, speechless. Their sorrow hung like cobwebs in the air.

After the funeral, my classmates began talking about the dead. They seemed to be boasting about the number of crash victims they had seen.

'Did you see their twisted faces?' they asked each other.

'Some of the dead were found hanging from the trees,' said another.

And then this one: 'Did you know that the balls of so-and-so were crushed?'

The wreckage of the C-47 was retrieved and left in the middle of the cogon fields in front of the apartment where we lived.

On stormy nights, we thought we could hear them, mostly the female voices carried by the wind: 'Help, please help us!'

Then: 'We are falling, we are falling! JesusMaryJoseph, please save us!'

I would grip my grandmother's arm; her rosary wound around her other hand, she would mutter her prayers. I was sure that the other people, both within our household and in the entire row of apartments beside ours, heard the voices in the night. But nobody dared talk about it when morning came.

It was a bright and windless summer day, a year after the airplane crash, when I decided to learn to ride my bike. My cousin taught me how to balance myself. 'Just look ahead of you,' he said. I did that. I fell and got bruised but, filled with determination and grit, in a week's time, I could ride the bike. I was riding with my friends when we reached the cogon fields. It was already late afternoon and a sickly light hung over the place. Suddenly, in the air rose the fragrance of frangipani flowers, the funeral flowers. My friends and I exchanged terrified glances and then we raced back to our houses. We avoided going near the cogon fields for the rest of that summer.

But the following summer, we decided to fly our kites. We were flying our diamond-shaped kites when the wind carried them in the direction of the cogon fields. Not wanting to lose the kites that we had made with our own hands, we followed the strings into the middle of the fields. The wind kept tugging my kite in one direction. I ran and ran, and when I stopped, I was already right in front of the wreckage of the C-47. We were surrounded by cogon grass. The aluminium wings of the plane glinted in the sun. I drew closer, drawn by its silvery sheen, when I saw a zipper stuck in the wingtip. In a flash, I was gone.

* * *

When my grandfather died, it was my two sisters' turn to stay home in our house in Antipolo. My mother and I returned to Albay. It was a hot afternoon when my grandfather was buried. So long was the cortège which snaked around the town that I thought the entire town had turned up for his funeral. I was holding on to my mother, who was weeping. I loved my mother very much and it was difficult to hear her weeping. If only I could do anything to stop her from shedding her tears, I would have already done it. I had to restrain her when she lunged towards my grandfather's coffin as it was being pushed into the niche.

At that exact same moment, my sisters told me later, something strange happened in our house. My sisters were in their bedroom. Suddenly the white curtains lifted on that windless day, and a chill spread through the room. My sisters held each other's hands, whispering, 'Grandfather, grandfather,' and then, they began to sob. When we returned home, silent in our grief, our house looked empty and suddenly old.

Years—many years—later, I was trying to survive my first winter in Scotland as a postgraduate student in publishing studies when, one night, I dreamed about my *ninong*, my godfather. He lived a few houses away from our house in Basa Air Base, Pampanga. In my dream, I seemed to be in a room shaped like a box. The room had an open ceiling, and my ninong was peering down from the roof. His eyes were sad. The next morning, I got a letter from my father. He also attached a newspaper obituary about my ninong's death. I wrote to my *ninang*, my godmother, and told her about my dream. She answered that my ninong had died peacefully in his sleep.

A year later, I saw Pita, my ninong's daughter. She said that during the height of the Mount Pinatubo eruption, she went to Villamor Air Base gym to see what she could do for the residents of Basa Air Base. Our air base was only 10 kilometres from Mount Pinatubo. The volcano's ashes had destroyed the roof of the hangar, as well as many other houses in the airbase. The residents of the air base had been evacuated to Villamor Air Base by C-130 cargo planes.

Then Pita met a woman who knew her family. She said to Pita, 'It's good to see you. You know, your father was also here a while ago. He was so kind. He was asking us what he could do to help us.'

Astonished, Pita said, 'But Papa had died a year ago.'

The woman just looked at Pita and simply dissolved into tears.

* * *

When I got word that I had received a writer's grant to stay at Hawthornden Castle in Midlothian, Scotland, I was so happy. But I was also wary. I was happy because I could begin writing my first novel. But I was also wary because I didn't want to stay in Boswell Room. Eric Gamalinda, one of my friends, had stayed there and swore he had seen a ghost—a woman in white—at the foot of his bed. In his mind, he told her that if she didn't go away, he would zap her with a mantra. The woman vanished.

To my dismay, I was assigned the Boswell Room for a month. During my first night, I was just too tired from the twenty-hour flight from Manila to Heathrow Airport, in London, followed by the six-hour train journey from London to Scotland. I dragged my blue suitcase up the narrow, winding stairs, up to the fourth storey of the castle. When I reached my room, I just collapsed on my bed and fell asleep.

At dawn the next morning, I saw a woman in white approaching my bed. Her long hair streamed down from her head. I thought she was Margaret, the cook, but then remembered the photos in the brochure that Margaret was fat. Then I thought she was Effie, the housekeeper, but then remembered that Effie had short hair. So, who was this woman gliding towards me in what seemed like nanoseconds? I wanted to scream but thought that that would be too embarrassing. When you represent your country overseas, you have to restrain yourself from such ungracious behaviour. So, I just kept quiet as she approached. She seemed to be checking who I was. When she drew close to me, I saw that she had no face— only a blank darkness. I screamed. In a flash she was gone. I must have startled her as well because she flew and slammed into the wall. The last thing I saw was the tail of her long hair vanishing into the heavy, wooden door.

The next day, we had a heavy breakfast of sausages and eggs, Quaker oats and sliced apples. After eating, I went to both Margaret and Effie in the kitchen and asked them if there was, indeed, a ghost in the Scottish castle? They told me that something happened in the castle more than three hundred years ago. There used to be a lady in the castle named Fiona Cunningham. Fiona was supposed to marry William Drummond, the *laird*, or lord, of the castle. But since he had blue blood and she was a mere commoner, his relatives, naturally, objected to the marriage. A few days before the wedding, she was found dead on the lookout ledge of the castle, overlooking the River Esk. Somebody must have poisoned the poor woman. Lord Drummond was inconsolable with grief, and never married.

I do not know why she haunts that place still. Hawthornden Castle is perched on an ancient rock and seems to be floating on leaves in varying tints of green. I suppose if you were about to marry the person you loved and were poisoned instead, wouldn't you do the same—look into each face, examine everyone, try to find the one who killed you, so you could bring the murderer to that place of your exile—that place of utter darkness and grief?

When I studied in the United States, I lived in a very old house near Rutgers University in New Brunswick, New Jersey. It was also a house of the spirits. But that is a story for another day.

CHILD OF THE
ASH-COVERED SKY

This tale is for National Artist Rolando S. Tinio

Lindo was a boy of eleven and the only thing he wanted was to have blue eyes and white skin.

'Mama, why are my eyes as black as shadows and my skin as brown as mud?' He would sometimes ask his mother this question ever since he began to speak. After explaining to Lindo several times that Filipinos had black eyes and brown skin, his mother grew tired of the question.

Lindo liked watching *Captain America* and *Superman* on the telly. They were bigger than any Filipino he had seen, stronger surely, and why, Superman could even fly!

He also liked watching *Sesame Street* every day and had acquired an American accent.

One day, Mount Pinatubo, an old volcano on the western side of Luzon Island, exploded for the first time in 500 years. People had assumed that it was an extinct volcano. But, like people, volcanoes seem to have hidden lives as well.

Lindo remembers the day, still sharp in his mind's eye, even if it had already happened many years ago. He was running around in their backyard bordered with blooming bougainvillea at around five o'clock in the afternoon. Air seemed to have been sucked out of that day; it was very hot, indeed. Suddenly, he felt something hit his eye. He quickly wiped his eyes, but the thing stayed in his eye. It felt like the grain of something, and it made his eyes itch. He was still trying to get the grain out of his eye when his mother came out to the backyard, running.

'We should go inside now, Lindo. Mount Pinatubo has just exploded!' He could hear a tremor in his mother's voice, something he had never heard before. He quietly allowed her to lead him by the hand. He told him about the grain in his eye. She brought him into the bathroom and washed his face and eyes. They went back to the living room, where he sat on a sofa with orange upholstery. The telly was on and he could hear a frantic broadcaster giving his live report.

'As you can see, we will now enter our van and leave the site of the volcano. There is a mushroom cloud above it now and it is spewing black smoke and white sand into the sky. We will literally run for our lives now!' And then he was gone.

Lindo's mother prepared his favourite hamburger with its real tomato sauce, not the sweet banana sauce that his classmates and neighbours used. Even his sauce was imported from the USA. As he was eating, his father arrived and kissed his mother on the left cheek. He also kissed Lindo on the forehead and ruffled his son's hair.

His parents sat transfixed in front of the telly in its brown, wooden case. Usually, after watching a show, they would go to the television set, turn it off and draw the shutters of its case closed.

However, today they seemed to be watching not just one but several news shows, one after the other. They featured the same scenes of panic-stricken people, running for their lives carrying nothing but the clothes on their backs. There was also a long queue of Americans in their cars, leaving Subic and Clark, the two American military bases near the exploding volcano.

After his meal, Lindo quietly slipped out of the house. The backyard was already dark. The moon looked like a yellow scythe in the sky. But he noticed something falling very slowly. A fine film of white and powdery sand was drifting down over everything. He first felt it before he realized that it was very fine sand. It fell silently on his hair and forehead and cheeks, on his shoulders and body and feet. It felt like a breathing being, deadly and invisible, blowing sand onto him until he was completely covered in white.

When he entered their house, his parents gaped at him.

'Now, I have to give you a bath, Lindo. That's the powdery sand from the volcano. It has turned you completely white!'

Lindo wished that his mother would not wash away the white powder that coated his body, covering his brown skin. Now the only thing that remained was to wait to be older, so he could buy blue contact lenses. He had seen the adverts on the telly, how one's black eyes could turn into magical and beautiful blue.

It was in this state of hopefulness that he slept well that night. His window was open and unbeknownst to him, the volcano continued to erupt all night long, spewing billions of sand grains, as fine as powder and as white as snow over a vast area. The particles floated over everything and smothered the Philippines as well as many parts of Southeast Asia.

The volcanic ash also drifted into Lindo's bedroom. It fell on Lindo throughout the night around his body asleep on his bed. When he woke up in the morning, everything was white: his clothes in their hangers, the brown-painted dresser, the parquet floor. And when he stood up and looked at his bed, his body was outlined on his bed. Invisible fingers seemed to have poured many grains of powdery sand around his sleeping form.

When he walked out of his room—their house, the front yard, and the steel gate, the whole wide world was already shrouded in white, like a graveyard.

PARABLE OF SUMMER NO. 2:
THE SEA

The sky is as wide and as blue as the sea, Bien thought, when their motorcycle stopped under the shade of a tall coconut tree on the beach. Bien jumped off the motorcycle, his slippers landing on the milky-white grains of sand. When he began to walk, his slippers left footprints on the sand, like wounds.

'Okay. You should change into your swimming trunks now so that we can swim,' his father said. His voice was unusually cold, like the sea breeze now blasting before him.

'Yes, Father. But I had really hoped that Mother would be with us today,' he said sadly.

'Oh, she's busy doing so many things today. Don't you want to be with me today? I will teach you how to swim!'

'Yes! I'd like that,' Bien exclaimed, the joy back in his words.

After a while, the two had changed into their swimming trunks. His father wore black trunks, while Bien wore blue. The sand grains were already aflame when Bien ran towards the water. A chill knifed through him at the first touch of the sea water on his body. But he soon got used to the cold. His father ran after him. The waves dashed themselves against the black and craggy rocks.

'You should not be afraid of the water if you ever want to learn to swim,' his father told Bien. 'Come here. First sit on my shoulders.'

Bien sloshed through the water until he reached his father. The older man crouched and Bien jumped on to his broad shoulders. His father held Bien's ankles. Bien gripped his father's neck. When he looked up, he thought: this sky is bluer than the colour of the marbles that I played with my neighbours.

Then Bien's father slowly stood up and began wading through the water. The waves dashed themselves again on the black and craggy rocks. Bien was surprised when saw the water turning deeper. 'Father, I'm afraid of the deep water,' he said.

'Oh, that's only water,' his father answered. His voice was cold, like the sea breeze now blasting stronger before them.

And then he continued to walk.

When the water reached his father's chin, Bien's legs were already knee-deep in the water. The boy felt that his father's grip on his ankles seemed to have gotten tighter.

Bien wanted to scream, but his father spoke, 'Your uncle Julian is right—there is mud under the sea.'

And he continued to walk.

'Uncle Julian!' Bien wanted to call out, remembering his uncle who sometimes visited them on weekends, bringing him his favourite purple yam ice cream.

But his father began to speak again, 'And the sea is also impotent—'

Bien began to cry when the water reached his father's nose. But his father just continued to walk.

Bien began to scream when the water reached his father's hair. He raised his eyes to the sky, but it remained mute. The last thing he saw was the sky, as blue as the marbles he played with in their backyard.

His father turned into a black and craggy rock, buried in the graveyard of the sea. But Bien, he just swam and swam, beside the silver jellyfish and the spotted whale, surrounded by sea anemones and green seaweeds, now far away from sadness, and from fear.

THE FIREFLIES

This tale is for Mark Brownrigg

It had been a strange week in this village on top of the Antipolo hills. The days were cool, and night hid itself beneath a thick, woollen blanket.

However, I liked this change in the weather, so different from the hot and humid weather before where the sweat stuck on you like a second skin. After dinner of hot chicken *tinola*, the taste of chicken soup with sliced ginger and pepper leaves still on my tongue, I went out of the house. I walked to the front yard. Tonight, I immediately placed the fragrance floating in our garden. It came from the white jasmine called *dama de noche*, the lady of the night, standing beside our high, steel gate. It seemed to be waiting for a friend.

I walked toward the dama de noche, my head in a daze as I inhaled its fragrance. I felt my body becoming light. It was then that I noticed the three fireflies, like lamps glowing around the small, white flowers.

At the sight of the fireflies, I immediately ran to our kitchen to get an empty glass jar. Slowly and silently, I tiptoed towards the dama de noche. The fireflies' tiny bodies blazed around the twigs, flowers and leaves.

With bated breath, I quickly scooped the three fireflies into the jar. One of them managed to escape. But the other two, trapped in the jar, continued to fly, their bodies bumping blindly against the glass. When they got tired, they slowly settled at the bottom of the jar and rested. Immediately, I secured the jar's mouth with a piece of white cloth gripped with a rubber band.

I was humming to myself when I stepped into the house. I put the jar on the low table beside my bed. I suddenly felt tired and drowsy. I decided to go to sleep. I pulled the string of the lampshade and darkness fell in my room. I had assumed that the fireflies would continue to glow in the dark, but they did not. I wanted them to burn just as brightly in my dark room as they had done outside, in the perfumed garden. I knocked on the cold, hard glass of the jar, grabbed it and jiggled it this way and that. But still, no more fire came from the insect's bodies.

Wearily, I dropped off to sleep.

* * *

Once upon a time, the young king of Arcadia lost his diamond ring. He loved his ring very much because it had been given to him as a gift by his mother, the queen, when the king had been a child.

The words of the Queen Mother still rang in his ears: 'You can only wear this ring after you've been crowned king.'

His father, the king, died at the age of sixty. As he was beloved by the people, the whole kingdom grieved at his passing. On everyone's faces fell a dark veil.

Exactly a month after burying the king, it was the queen's turn to die. People said she must have missed the king, and she died of sadness. Sharp and bitter were the tears of the prince when he laid his mother to rest. She had always had time for him—she had read stories to him when he was very young and had shown him how love could be possible in this world. On the other hand, the king had always been busy with affairs of the state and with slaying the invaders from the arctic North.

Seeing the weeping prince, the whole kingdom realized that, yes, sadness does not spare even those who were blue of blood. To lessen his loneliness, the prince began seeing again a young woman who had been his friend since childhood. She was the baker's only daughter. On her the prince seemed to still smell the fragrance of freshly baked bread. She had a mole on her right cheek, a mole as round as a small coin. As the days passed by, the prince and the baker's daughter knew that they were beginning to fall in love. He loved this woman, calm and cool as a river. In turn, she loved him, too, and wanted to save him from his sadness.

They knew they needed each other to feel the depth of life.

The kingdom exploded with joy when they were married a week after the prince had become the king.

'The king has married a commoner,' they exclaimed, and yet, nobody complained. Even the gossips shut up and continued looking for lice in each other's hair.

Now, together, the newly married couple felt that they could fully savour the colour and texture of life. They could hold their love up, like wine against the light.

Now, together, they could face life's gladness and grief. But one month after their wedding, the king lost his ring, the one that the Queen Mother had given to him. He combed the room, the meandering hallway, the great hall. No ring. He asked the palace hands to look for it. But still, there was no ring. So, one day, the king issued a royal bulletin. It was written in script, tacked on doors and announced in the public squares by the royal barkers: 'Anybody who can find the king's diamond ring will have his dreams fulfilled.'

New blood seemed to have been pumped into the kingdom's veins. Everyone looked high and low for the diamond ring—the rich, who wanted to become richer; the poor, who wanted to have some measure of comfort. Even the birds and the worms, the grasshoppers and the butterflies, looked for the ring.

One day, a firefly crawled towards the king who was sitting on his mauve throne.

'Your highness,' said the firefly with a deep bow, 'I have finally found your ring.'

'Where is it, my dear firefly?' asked the king, instantly rising from the soft seat of his throne.

'Please come with me tonight, your highness,' the firefly answered.

* * *

It had been a strange week. The days were cool and the nights hid beneath a thick, woollen blanket. But the king did not mind the change in weather. In fact, he liked it because the several layers of clothing he always wore made him feel comfortable and warm. That night, he went with the firefly into the garden. They stopped in front of a high, steel gate.

A fragrance floated in the garden, the fragrance of dama de noche. The king seemed to go into a daze as he inhaled the fragrance, his body becoming inexplicably light. He only snapped out of his reverie when the firefly spoke.

'Your highness,' it said, 'your diamond ring is up there, atop the dama de noche. It fell from your finger one night when you stopped in front of the flowers to inhale their fragrance. I climbed the dama de noche myself and placed the ring on top so that no one else could claim to have found it.'

The king looked up. The ring, indeed, was there: a small star amidst the spangle of flowers. One of the palace hands climbed up the dama de noche and retrieved the ring.

'So, now, pray tell me, what do you want for yourself? What dreams do you want me to fulfil?'

'Just two dreams, your highness—first, I want to have wings of gossamer so that I can fly faster. And second, I wish . . . I wish to have light inside my body.'

The king's jaw dropped.

The firefly groped for words, 'Please don't see anything bad in my second wish, your highness. I want to have a glowing body not because I want to compete with the king's ring, or with the queen's jewelled crown; I only want a lamp for my body . . . so I won't get lost when I travel in the dark. You see, your highness, I always visit my friends at night.'

The king's face lit up. Then he said, 'Fine, my dearest firefly. From now on, your two wishes will come true. From now on, all your kith and kin will have the gift of flight. And your bodies will also glow in the dark.'

'Thank you so much, your highness,' said the firefly. He wanted to kiss the feet of the king or even the hem of his purple robes. But the king forbade him.

'I'm the one who owes you a debt of gratitude for finding the ring that the Queen Mother had given to me. I hope you'll be happy from now on.'

The moment the king turned away and began walking to the palace, the firefly felt something growing inside him. It was something fine, like gossamer or gauze, sprouting from the sides of his body. When he looked around, he saw a speck of light begin to glow on his tail. The warm speck became a body of light, a comet streaking all over him, until the shimmer reached his very face.

He felt warm and buoyant. He felt that he could do anything. So, he flapped one wing, then the other. He did this again and again. Faster and faster. His body slowly lifted from the dead weight of the ground. And he began to fly.

'Now, I can visit my friends even at night!' shouted the firefly as he began to fly in the cold darkness covering the land.

Ending No. 1:

His voice resonated round the garden, jumped over the thick walls of the palace, floated over the years, the centuries, the different zones of time, until it spilt over into a home ablaze with lights. Cold and hard was the glass on top of me. My small fingers touched the rectangle of glass on my face. I tried to push it away so I could breathe, but the glass lying over me was cold and hard.

Ending No. 2:

His voice resonated round the garden, jumped over the thick walls of the palace, floated over the years, centuries, the different zones of time, until it spilt over into a home ablaze with lights.

I woke up with a start. Even though the night was cool, I found my back still soaked with sweat. I tugged at the string of the lampshade, and light drenched my room immediately.

I rose from my bed and then, I saw the fireflies. They were very still inside the glass jar.

They must be dead! I thought, my heart beating fast. The whole house was still asleep. Even though I was mortally afraid of being alone in the dark, I stepped out of my room. The glass jar was in my hand. Some inner voice seemed to be telling me to go out. I unlocked the kitchen door.

The chill of the night gave me goose pimples. But the dama de noche was still there, spilling its perfume into the air, waiting for a friend to drink in its fragrance.

I walked towards the small, white flowers. The night was so still, all I could hear was my own breathing.

I stopped in front of the dama de noche, gripping the jar tightly. I snapped the rubber band and took away the cloth covering the mouth of the jar.

The cold wind crawled into the jar. I saw the fireflies slowly stir from their sleep. Their gossamer wings began to move. Soon, specks of light began to glow on their tails. The specks became bodies of light, comets streaking all over them, until the shimmer reached their very faces.

I rubbed my knuckles against my eyes. I felt warm and buoyant. I felt I could do anything.

The fireflies slowly floated and left their glass tomb. 'I hope that you'll see your friends again. I hope that you'll be happy,' I said to the fireflies as they floated like heartbeats lighting the night air.

In return, the fireflies flapped their wings as a gesture of both farewell and gratitude. Now they could roam in the vast world. At last, they were again free.

Please choose your own ending.

APPENDIX

Litro Magazine, New York City, interviews Danton Remoto.
This interview appeared in the 27 November 2021
issue of the magazine.

For this instalment of 'A Flash of Inspiration' we're featuring 'The Snake', a story by Danton Remoto that originally appeared in *Litro Magazine*, New York City, on 29 January 2021.

Litro: How long have you been writing fiction? Do you write in other genres? Do you find that you return to certain themes in your writing?

Danton Remoto: I have been writing fiction since my university days in the early 1980s. My first creative writing teacher was the late Professor Emmanuel Torres at the Jesuit-run Ateneo de Manila University. Professor Torres went to school at the Iowa Writers' Workshop and was a classmate of Robert Bly. One day, Bly allegedly brought a snake to school on the day his poem was to be discussed in the workshop. Paul Engle, the professor, and all of the students couldn't say anything negative about Robert Bly's poem. I was also lucky to have Philippine National Artist Edith L. Tiempo as a mentor in fiction-writing at the Silliman University Writers' Workshop. She also studied at the Iowa Writers' Workshop under Robert Penn Warren. I attended the Bread Loaf Writers' Conference in 2019 and took the fiction-writing workshop conducted by the marvellous Tiphanie Yanique. I write poetry as well; in fact, I have three books of poems that have won awards in the Philippines. However, I am most prolific in writing essays. I have been writing a column for the Philippine press since 1990; this year marks the thirty-first year of my column-writing. I have published seven books of essays. All of my books were first written in English.

Yes, I do find that certain themes recur in all the genres that I write. These are the themes of departure and return, the character or persona going back to a place or a memory or a country and then returning to the present; love and its shadow, which is loss, like the two sides of the moon; and the struggles and resistance that we have to endure as people living in a developing, postcolonial country.

Litro: What inspired the writing of 'The Snake'?

DR: I lived in Singapore in the summer of 2003 as a research fellow on Asian Literature at the globally ranked National University of Singapore (NUS). I got a grant from the Asian Scholarship Foundation funded by Ford Foundation. I lived in a high-end condominium in Simei with two other Filipinos, who were well paid in their respective jobs. Simei was at the other end of the island from the university so, every day, I took two trains to get to the university. I would mostly see tall buildings and beautiful condominiums on the way to the university. I knew that Singapore, like Malaysia where I had also lived, used to be heavily forested. But the forest cover was mostly gone, in the rush to progress. But could we really banish nature? Could we make it disappear such that no remnants or relics would appear to remind us of the forest that used to cover the land? In Freudian fashion, the forest here could also signify the world of the subconscious that we try to suppress with our busy and modern lives. Or it could also mean the rich and moist world of the creative process, where the words whirl and form.

Litro: I find that you do an excellent job of balancing acute social analysis in 'The Snake' with empathy and a light touch. Was this a challenging line to walk?

DR: Thank you for your kind words. Yes, indeed, it was difficult to write. It was a piece of flash fiction that was less than 500 words, but it took me months to write it. I also had conversations with some of my writer friends in Singapore and read widely on its literature, which was part of my research fellowship at NUS. I wanted to write a very short story that was also a piece of social analysis. But I always try to avoid heavy-handed writing. In my mind, a feather's touch could also be deadly, like the small green snake coiled at the bottom of the toilet bowl in the penthouse of an expensive condo in Singapore.

Litro: Who was the reader you had in mind when you conceived this story?

DR: When I write, I really do not think of a particular reader. The first reader is obviously me, and I try to revise all of my work to as fine a degree as possible. I wrote this piece almost twenty years ago, as I said, when I was doing research on Asian literature. So perhaps subconsciously, my first readers would be my fellow Asians who are torn between tradition and modernity, and then any other readers who would stumble upon the work. That is why I was so delighted when *Litro Magazine* in New York City published it with hardly any editorial revision at all.

Litro: Tell us about some of your writing preferences. Pen, pencil or computer? Language or plot? First, second or third person? Male or female protagonist? Short forms or long forms?

DR: I now use my laptop computer. I am old now, but I remember writing using my blue ballpoint pen, then a white Olympia manual typewriter that used to belong to my father, an entrepreneur.

In fiction, I first think of the character. I have to hear his or her voice before I can start a word of the work. I usually write in the first person, with mostly male protagonists. But I have finished two novels, *Riverrun*, published by Penguin Random House Southeast Asia, and *The Country of Desire*, which I am still revising. My third novel will also use the first-person point of view.

But for my fourth novel, I might finally use the third-person point of view. It will be a historical novel about Southeast Asia, to be written with 'empathy and a light touch, but with an acute social analysis', as you put it. I have also finished a book of short stories called *The Heart of Summer: Stories and Tales*. This book gathers together the short fiction I have written over the last thirty years. Some of the stories were written in the realistic mode; others are fantasy stories. But now, I am drawn to writing novels. It is like creating a vast, new world whose characters move according to your will, people with their own fears and dreams.

Litro: What do you feel are the biggest challenges of writing a successful piece of flash fiction?

DR: I think the biggest challenge in writing flash fiction is how to make sure that the conflict is already there at the outset. My technique is to think of flash fiction as a short film. With a few deft scenes, you should have already put in place the character and the conflict, and let the story take over. Using this technique of flash fiction as a short film ensures that it is anchored on a series of moving and poetic images. In flash fiction, the story moves, but on the wings of song.

Litro: How do you combat bad writing habits and stay motivated?

DR: I procrastinate a lot before I actually write, but when I do, the images or voices in the story live inside me for days. When I am in the midst of writing a novel, I even dream of the scenes I had written, or the scenes that I have yet to write. It's as if my subconscious is helping me write this work that is already like a fully ripened fruit in my mind. The actual writing takes place after I have done my research and I can already hear the voice of the main character. My third novel is about a Filipino studying in New Jersey and living in New York City in the year 2001 when the Twin Towers collapsed. But even though I lived there during that time, I had to do a lot of research on the streets, the buildings, the locations of the Asian restaurants, the things found in Chinatown, etc. I am a self-propulsive writer. I wasn't the best writer in school when I studied at Jesuit-run university in Manila, or at the University of Stirling in Scotland, or at Rutgers University in New Jersey, but I think I was the one who kept on writing. The best university writers have become rich doctors and lawyers, but here I am, still writing almost forty years after I finished my university degree.

Litro: Where do you turn for creative inspiration? Which writers (and/or stories) are particularly important to you? What books of note are you currently reading?

DR: I think of my country, the Philippines, when I write, its beauty and poverty, as well as its complex history; I think of my past, as an Asian of Malay-Chinese-Spanish descent educated in the United Kingdom and the United States; I think of that common reader in some library carrel or place near or far from me who might one day read my book. The Philippine National Artist, Nick Joaquin, and the Philippine national hero, Dr Jose Rizal, whose novels *Noli me Tangere* and *El Filibusterismo*, led to his execution by firing squad by the Spaniards, are important to me. When I first read *One Hundred Years of Solitude* by Gabriel Garcia Marquez, I was shocked because it sounded like the tales told by my grandmother. Some of its pages also looked like the unreported news of death and violence under our homegrown dictatorship. I did not know that a novel could be written like this! *The Art of the Novel* by Milan Kundera was helpful in teaching me the structure of the novel. The fairy tales of Angela Carter in *The Bloody Chamber and Other Stories* are lodestars, as is the fiction of Jayne Ann Phillips in *Black Tickets and Other Stories*. The poetry of Carolyn Forché in *The Country Between Us* and *Gathering the Tribes*, as well as the vivid poems of the T'ang Dynasty masters Li Po,

Wang Wei and Tu Fu helped shape my writing as well. And of course, the lyrical poems of Pablo Neruda still sing to me. All these beautiful poems seem to have been painted with words.

Litro: What are you working on now?

DR: I have just finished a book of poems called *The Country of Memory*. I am also thinking of writing my memoirs since people said I have lived an interesting life—from founding what CNN has called the first LGBTQ+ political party in the world, Ladlad (Coming Out) Party List, to writing during a time of a dictatorship and military coups. I am also writing my third novel now. On the surface it looks like a light and breezy gay romance novel, but beneath it simmers the issues of race, immigration and the diaspora. I hope to make it entertaining as well.

ACKNOWLEDGEMENTS

Some of these short stories and tales have been published in the following periodicals: *Asia Pacific Writers and Translators Bengaluru Review*, *Focus Philippines*, *Heights*, *Katitikan: A Journal of Southern Philippines*, *Litro Magazine New York*, *Metro Magazine Summer Reading Fiction Issue*, *National Midweek*, *Philippine Graphic*, *Philippines Free Press*, *Philippine Star*, *The Blue Tiger Review U.S.A.* and *The Manila Times*. I would like to thank the editors who first published them: Kerima Polotan, Gregorio Brillantes, Nick Joaquin, Jocelyn de Jesus, Catherine McNamara, Millet Mananquil, Thelma Sioson San Juan, Ryan Thorpe and Thomas Leonard Shaw. The other stories in this collection are being published for the first time.

'Parable of Summer #2: The Sea' won the first prize in the Short Story Competition at the Stirling District Council Literary Awards, United Kingdom.

'The Heart of Summer' won the second prize at the *Philippines Free Press* Literary Awards while 'Wings of Desire' won the third prize at the *Philippine Graphic* Literary Awards.

I would like to thank the James and Mary Mulvey Fellowship Grant and the University Research Council of Ateneo de Manila University for their support during the writing of some stories in this book.

My eternal gratitude goes to Professor Emmanuel Torres, my first mentor in creative writing, whose late afternoon classes at the Ateneo Art Gallery are forever imprinted in my memory.

I would like to thank the formidable Kerima Polotan for publishing my early stories in her weekly magazine, *Focus Philippines*. I am indebted to Dr Lourdes Salvador, the director of the Asian Scholarship Foundation, which gave me two research scholarships to read Asian Literature at the Universiti Kebangsaan Malaysia (National University of Malaysia) and the National University of Singapore. I also spent my spare time in Malaysia and Singapore reading fiction and writing some of the stories in this book.

Moreover, a British Council scholarship at the University of Stirling as well as a Fulbright scholarship at Rutgers University gave me the time to read fiction, both short- and long-form, as well as write some of the stories in this collection. Special thanks go to my sister, Nanette Remoto, whose home in Los Angeles was a haven for the writing of fiction as well as a respite from the 'the excess of reality' that I sometimes experience in the Philippines.

My eternal gratitude goes to my eye doctor, Dr Noel Lacsamana of the International Eye Centre in San Fernando, Pampanga, Philippines. He did cataract surgery and lasik surgery on my eyes, allowing me to see the world in a new and brilliant light.

I would also like to thank Nora Nazerene Abu Bakar of Penguin Random House Southeast Asia for her sharp editorial instinct, as well as her hardworking editorial and marketing staff, for believing in the words that I write. It still thrills me to know that my first novel, *Riverrun*, also published by Penguin Random House Southeast Asia, is being sold in all the major and independent booksellers worldwide, in both online as well as mortar-and-brick bookstores.

The Heart of Summer was completed during the strict COVID-19 lockdowns in Malaysia and the Philippines that lasted for more than two years. I would like to thank my partner, James Tuñacao, for taking care of me during my stay in Cebu, where I survived an accident and later, a Category 5 tropical cyclone that lashed Central Visayas and Northern Mindanao in December of 2021.

I revised this book at the MacDowell Artists' Residency in New Hampshire, U.S.A., in the happy summer of 2022. Thank you to my kind and talented cohorts, especially to Peng Zuqiang, who provided great conversation and company.

And thank you, universe, for another book.

PRAISE FOR 'RIVERRUN,
A NOVEL'

'*Riverrun* is a fine novel and Danton Remoto is a literary heavyweight.'

—*Vogue Australia*

'Set during the Marcos years, rich in childhood memories of local customs, myths and food. A compelling and entertaining coming-of-age memoir about a young Filipino man's discovery of his sexuality.'

—Suchen Christine Lim, Winner of the Singapore Literature Prize and the Southeast Asian Write Award; Author of the novels, *Dearest Intimate* and *A River's Song*

'*Riverrun, A Novel* is a Filipino queer masterpiece. It has many scenes where the simple surface details hint at the tensions simmering underneath . . . Each scene feels small and intimate, the prose sticking to specifics even as it powerfully evokes everything from horror to comedy. We jump from moment to moment, each one with a luminous clarity that can be found in the best poetry . . . Remoto is one of the editors of the *Ladlad* literary anthologies—*ladlad* meaning "unfurled, to come out"—as well as the founder of the Ladlad Party List, an LGBT political party that was denied participation in the Philippine elections on grounds of "immorality . . ." Remoto often serves his societal critiques with a generous dash of hilarity and witty irreverence. Altogether, a book of great lyricism and power.'

          —Global Literature in Libraries Initiative, New York City

'*Riverrun, A Novel* is one of the most anticipated LGBTQ+ novels of the year.'

          —Lambda Literary, New York City

'To read *Riverrun, A Novel* is to be beguiled by a storyteller at the height of his powers. Danton Remoto weaves the personal with the political, in prose that is deeply evocative, deliciously acid, and unflinchingly truthful.'

          —F.H. Batacan, author of the novel, *Smaller and Smaller Circles*, winner of the Palanca and Madrigal Prizes for Literature

'*Riverrun* is a poignant tale from one of the pioneers of gay writing in the Philippines. It is a coming-of-age story that follows a young man growing up under the Philippine government's tyranny from the 1970s and the 1980s. This book is genre-bending. At times, it feels like a novel, but it also feels a memoir. It is one of the five most anticipated books by an Asian author for the year 2020.'

          —*Bookriot.com*, New York City

'*Riverrun* is an elegant and stirring novel. There is no magic realism here, but it all reminds you of Gabriel Garcia Marquez.'

          —*Book Matters*

'*Riverrun* is one of the best contemporary novels written in the Philippines in the last ten years.'

          —Alfred A. Yuson, *Philippine Star*

'*Riverrun, A Novel* is a delightful and poetic read, lightly trodden but deeply impactful; and indeed, as intended, it reads like a personal, intimate memoir.'

—Elaine Chiew, *Asian Books Blog*

'Danton Remoto writes with clarity and depth. *Riverrun, A Novel* is a fine and vivid exploration into the human heart. It is also a passionate excoriation of those who have turned the country into a prison house.'

—*The Manila Times*

'*Riverrun, A Novel* is a riveting story of a young man in a military dictatorship in the Philippines. The grimness and the violence are leavened by its wicked wit and sly humour, as well as by its form, which is that of a memoir. This pastiche of a novel is never cut-and-dried. Instead, it is a warm and large-hearted work that should win many new readers for Danton Remoto in Asia, and the rest of the world.'

—Malachi Edwin Vethamani, Author of *Coitus Interruptus and Other Stories*; Editor of *Ronggeng-Ronggeng: Malaysian Short Stories*

'*Riverrun A Novel* succeeds as an honest portrayal of coming to terms with one's sexuality. It is organized as a series of fine vignettes, with the writing pared down to resemble the drips of a faucet... The fragmented structure gives Remoto the opportunity to employ a heightened sense of observation, giving each and every moment a sense of daily detail that coming-of-age writing rarely achieves. As one finishes this welcome addition to the growing library of gay novels, one has the impression of having lived life alongside Danilo.'

—Kiran Bhat, *Asian Review of Books*

'*Riverrun A Novel* is an intimate read for rainy nights like these. It is also rich with incidents on history and politics, but they are never preachy. Moreover, food is a pervasive element in the novel, working like a Greek chorus that comments on the sad and funny scenes. Danton Remoto's wonderful novel now sits firmly on a global platform, where it deserves to be.'

—CNN Philippines

'*Riverrun, A Novel* is a unique and idiosyncratic book. It runs, river-like, along a gentle narrative arc . . . Through small, often lovely quotidian moments at home and in school, as his family moves from rural Pampanga to urban Quezon City, and beyond, who Danilo is and what he wants in life is revealed to the reader . . . It works as a novel, simultaneously romantic and exotic, both in story and in language. Frequently, the turn of phrase in the pieces may sometimes strike readers as strange, slightly foreign in some instances, the way new music sounds at first hearing. In cadence, word choice and usage, it is unmistakably Filipino English—as the protagonist would actually speak it if you were to meet him . . . There are many hypnotic liquid lines that wash over you, gliding like water with music and sensuality. These are sentences wrought by someone clearly at home with the work of words . . . In *Riverrun*, the novelist has crafted something invitingly, insistently and seductively readable, and in that reading, he brings us genuine pleasure and joy alongside real pathos.'

—Noelle Q. De Jesus, *Esquire Magazine*

'Danton Remoto is a brilliant writer.'
      —Carolyn Ferrell, Shortlisted for the PEN Faulkner Award
            and the PEN Hemingway Award for the novel,
                              Dear Miss Metropolitan

'What makes Danton Remoto's *Riverrun* more than just your usual coming-of-age novel is his keen use of language, willingness to experiment with both chapter length and the inclusion of recipes, and his ability to set the rites of growing up against the ominous backdrop of the Philippines' chaotic military dictatorship without veering into melodrama. Memoir-like, *Riverrun* is told from the perspective of Danilo Cruz, a boy who grows up in Marcos' Philippines. From the very beginning, *Riverrun* opens with Danilo becoming keenly aware of the beauty and power of words, a skill he displays throughout the remainder of his narration with astute, often witty observations of the world around him using poetic yet exact language to depict it. There is a great charm to his childhood innocence, the wonder of attending school and time spent listening to his parents [and house maid] regale him with songs and ghost stories. I was left particularly tickled by the inclusion of recipes, such as his grandmother's *laing* to *kinunut*, fiercely embracing the Filipino identity across food and art. Remoto's wry sense of humour also contributes to the power of this novel, with an entire chapter dedicated to recounting the ongoings of a Miss Universe contest . . . *Riverrun* remains a striking piece of writing that showcases Remoto's mastery of the English language and his ability to eke out unresolved childhood traumas and memories, all while balancing it with humour and an unabashed pride for Filipino culture. Succinct and precise in writing, *Riverrun* is the ideal bildungsroman for the modern reader on a slow afternoon, each chapter a self-contained short story in and of itself, and coming together to form a lush account of Filipino childhood.'

—*Bakchormeeboy.com*, Singapore

'Danton Remoto is a hugely talented writer with a stylish and lyrical prose. I'll put my bets on him.'

—Professor Francisco Arcellana,
National Artist for Literature, Philippines

'*Riverrun, A Novel* follows the coming-of-age story of a young gay man during a dictatorship. Balancing the troubles of big-picture politics and intrapersonal anxieties, this memoir is filled with vignettes, poetry, flash fiction, and other literary forms that lead to a fun and touching read.'

—*Tatler Asia*

'In *The Art of Memoir*, Mary Karr describes memory as "a pinball in a machine—it messily ricochets around between image, fragments of scenes, and stories you've heard. Then the machine goes tilt and snaps off." That's what Danton Remoto uses to craft his most intimate novel, *Riverrun*. The form of the novel is a memoir and as the title suggests, the narrative runs gently like a river. This coming-of-age story is exquisitely told through vignettes, short prose, recipes, songs and poems. Remoto is a keen observer of people and situations. He has a way of presenting beautiful quotidian moments in a delicate manner . . . What I enjoy most are the folklore and mythologies that he weaves into his story, which add texture and layers to the novel . . . *Riverrun* has lyrical prose that is filled with such lovely details. It reminds me of reading a collection of creative nonfiction, and that's what makes this novel so unique and beautiful.'

—Yang Ming, *Ink Pantry*

'*Riverrun, A Novel* is a fun read; a must-buy book. And try the family recipes that are found in many of the chapters. Sumptuous.'
—Patricio Abinales, *Positively Filipino*

'Danton Remoto is the wonder boy of Philippine writing in English.'
—Dr Soledad S. Reyes, in her memoir, *Balik Tanaw: The Road Taken;* British Council Scholar on The Sociology of Literature, University of Essex

'*Riverrun, A Novel* is a swift, tender, sometimes rueful bildungsroman about a gay youth exploring the contours of his desires and the limits of his potential. The chapters traipse lightly but thoughtfully through the episodes of a life, with glancing social commentary and heartfelt recollections of defining relationships.'

—Cyril Wong, twice winner of the Singapore Literature Prize; author of the novel, *This Side of Heaven*

'*Riverrun, A Novel* belongs to the front list of contemporary gay novels in Asia.'

—Pink Alliance, Hong Kong

'Coming-of-age experiences aren't always the easiest to go through, much less in the middle of a dictatorship. But that's what the main character in *Riverrun* has to go through in this novel, which is a clever mix of flash fiction, poetry, and other forms of beautiful writing.'

—*Metro Scene* Magazine

'*Riverrun* is an elegant and exquisite novel that avoids the mawkish melodrama that is found in some Asian novels. I read it with pure delight.'

—Loy Arcenas, Winner of the Obie Award for Theatre, New York City

'The older I got, the novelists I like are those who write in short, concise sentences and who are also playful with their words . . . If you look at their sentences—very short, very brisk prose— yet, they say so much in so little. And the way they juxtapose words—a simple matter of changing a comma or putting a pause somewhere, and it changes the entire meaning of the sentence. I love that kind of literary play. I found these qualities in the works of Italo Calvino and Jeanette Winterson. It's something that I've also seen in *Riverrun, A Novel* by Danton Remoto. He says so much with so little. It takes mastery to have such an economy of language.'

—Marga Ortigas, ABS-CBN News Channel;
author of *The House on Calle Sombra: A Parable*